The Nine Bright Shiners

By Anthea Fraser

The Nine Bright Shiners)

ANTHEA FRASER

PUBLISHED FOR THE CRIME CLUB BY

Doubleday

NEW YORK

1988

All of the characters in this book
are fictitious, and any resemblance
to actual persons, living or dead,
is purely coincidental.

Library of Congress Cataloging-in-Publication Data

Fraser, Anthea
The nine bright shiners.

I. Title.
PR6056.R286N56   1988   823'.914   87-22365
ISBN 0-385-24323-5

Library of Congress Catalog Card Number

For my daughter Rosalind, with love.

The Nine Bright Shiners

CHAPTER 1

It lay at the back of a cupboard, huddled grotesquely like a lifeless old tramp. But the shabby jacket, the roll-neck sweater and grey flannels were padded with crumpled newspaper, and the face, staring from under a battered hat, was painted on a football.

In fact, the dummy resembled the guys which small boys throughout the country had prepared for Bonfire Night. But three things distinguished it, made it sinister. First, the cupboard where it was hidden did not belong to a small boy—and anyway Bonfire Night had passed. Second, nine green sequins had been incongruously sewn on a lapel. And third, in one of the frayed pockets was a pigskin wallet containing fifty pounds and a clutch of credit cards bearing the name of a highly respected citizen of the town.

Jan Coverdale handed her coffee-cup to the stewardess over the head of her sleeping daughter.

The girl gave her a friendly smile. "Going home for Christmas?"

Easier just to say "Yes," and in a way it was true. She'd be spending Christmas in the house where she was born, though her parents were no longer there and she scarcely knew her half-brother and his wife. Even so, Rylands would be more like home than the house in Sydney, without Roger. Her fingers clenched on the tray in front of her, and she registered the sidelong glance from her son. Consciously relaxing, she gave him a bright smile and pushed the tray up, securing it to the back of the seat in front.

Edward's letter had come as a surprise. He was almost a

stranger to her, more familiar on television than in real life, and she'd not expected any comment on the disintegration of her world. He was a busy man and she was, after all, twelve thousand miles away. Yet on receipt of her birthday card, with its pseudo-brave message that Roger had left them, came the invitation that was to catapult them into danger.

"We're sorry your marriage has broken down," he wrote, "and imagine Christmas is a bleak prospect. How would you like to spend it with us? We can't offer the weeks of sunshine you'd enjoy down there, but the children are at an age when a little old-world culture wouldn't go amiss, and you yourself would see quite a few changes after fifteen years."

He'd gone on to offer them the house for the eight-week Christmas holidays, even though he and Rowena would be flying to Peru before the New Year. And—the point that clinched it —he'd ended casually, "Needless to say, we'd cover the return fare for the three of you."

She hadn't hesitated. As he so accurately deduced, the approach of Christmas was her most immediate dread, and the inevitable "This time last year" would have less poignancy in wintry Broadshire. Also, she knew Roger would want to see the children over Christmas, which was an emotional hurdle they weren't ready for. And why should they be upset, simply to ease his conscience? she thought bitterly. He'd left them, as well as herself. Why should he come back when it suited him, smiling and bearing gifts as if nothing had happened?

The children themselves had offered no objections when told of the plan. Stunned by the abrupt departure of their father, their world was suddenly unsure, and the materialisation of relatives hitherto only names on a Christmas card offered a tenuous security.

But once her grateful acceptance had been posted came the doubts which, during sleepless nights, intensified to panic. What am I *thinking* of? she'd repeatedly asked herself. I don't *know* them *at all*. I don't know *anyone* there any more! Why fly halfway round the world to be with them?

It wasn't even as though she'd known Edward as a child. Ten

years her senior, he'd been at boarding school and university while she was growing up. And his wife, she felt, had never liked her. She'd always been there, on the fringe of Jan's childhood, as had Miles Coady. They were, after all, the daughter and son of her father's colleagues. Looking back, it was inevitable Rowena should have married either Edward or Miles.

Jan had found the wedding photo quite recently. It flattered none of them; Edward's eyes were shut, Rowena held her bouquet as though it were a machete, and she herself, their sixteen-year-old bridesmaid, was squinting against the sun. Only her parents seemed happy and relaxed, and it was because of them that she'd kept the picture.

She stirred, stretching her legs under the seat in front. The last time she'd seen them had been her own wedding-day, two days before she and Roger left for Australia. They'd been killed in a car crash five years later, while she was in hospital having her second baby. The house would be strange without them. They'd been such an integral part of it that she couldn't imagine anyone else living there, even Edward and Rowena.

"Why hasn't Uncle Edward any children?" Julie had inquired, as they were packing to come away.

"Because he's always out in the jungle, silly," Ben had retorted. Which saved Jan from giving what she felt was the true answer, that neither he nor Rowena cared for them.

"You must behave yourselves while we're there," she'd impressed on them, anxious that Edward shouldn't regret his possibly impulsive invitation.

"They'll be going to Peru soon anyway," Ben had said comfortably. Now, still perhaps mindful of her clenched fingers, he slid a small, warm hand inside hers, and she shook herself free of memories to smile at him.

"Tell me about Peru," he said. It was a plea for reassurance, and her heart constricted. It had been with tales of Peru that, from their earliest days, she had read her children to sleep, soothed their anxieties, and generally comforted them. Peru was, as it had been hers, their Never-Never Land, their Narnia, their Wonderland. Robin Hood was ousted by Atahualpa, and their nursery baddies were not King John and the Sheriff of Nottingham but the Spanish conquerors. At the same time, it was intensely personal folklore in which her own father had played his part. One of her most treasured possessions was a copy of his book, *The Hidden City*, which he'd inscribed "To my Inca Princess."

"Which story would you like?" she asked now, squeezing Ben's hand.

"The Third Expedition." But before she could begin, he twisted to face her. "Mum, why didn't you ever go to Peru?"

"By the time I was old enough, Grandpa'd stopped going."

"Why?"

Jan started to say he'd been too old, but that couldn't have been the reason. For neither her father nor Laurence Coady had returned to Peru after that third expedition in 1955. Of the three men who had taken part in it, only Reginald Peel, accompanied by his daughter Rowena and later by Edward, had continued to explore the country that had made them all famous.

"I don't know, Ben," she answered instead. As far as she herself was concerned, she had married at twenty and emigrated to Australia. A more pertinent question was why Miles Coady hadn't, like Edward and Rowena, followed in his father's footsteps. But Miles had never professed any interest in Peru. For the first time in years, she wondered where he was now, and what he had done with his life. At one time, he'd been interested in art.

"Go on, then," Ben prompted.

Jan spoke slowly, trying to find within the familiar story an answer to what, suddenly, she found puzzling. "Well, the three men set out from Cuzco in July 1955. They'd been planning the expedition for months, and were really looking forward to it. After the outstanding success of their last trip, they were convinced they'd be just as lucky this time. Laurence Coady had discovered there were still some descendants of Manco Inca living in a remote village in the Andes, and the aim was to trace them. But unfortunately, things started to go wrong almost at once. Their supplies were held up, which meant delaying their departure for several days. Then one of the mules went lame, and they had to abandon some provisions; and finally, after only ten days' walking, Grandpa developed a mysterious illness and had to be flown back to Lima."

"But the other two went on," Ben encouraged her, as she hesitated again.

"Yes." Jan tried to concentrate on the story. "After all these setbacks, they were more determined than ever for the expedition to succeed."

"And after losing their way lots of times, they finally found the village," Ben interjected, tired of waiting for her.

"Yes, and only just in time. The man was dying when they got there—he'd been shot by bandits."

"So it was all right in the end, wasn't it? They found what they were looking for, and Grandpa got better. Why didn't he write a book about that, too?"

"Because he'd no personal experience of it. He spent most of the time in hospital."

Was that why he'd never gone back to Peru? The bitter disappointment and frustration, after all the months of planning? But that was a risk in any expedition, and they'd had setbacks before. Why hadn't she asked him, while she still had the chance? Perhaps Edward would know.

"We could ask Uncle Edward," she said aloud, but Ben's eyes were drooping again and he didn't reply.

They landed at Heathrow at nine o'clock on a cold, drizzly morning, shivering and dazed from lack of sleep. Edward stood head and shoulders above the crowd in the Arrivals Hall, and from that distance his resemblance to her father was almost uncanny. As they moved forward with their trolley, still surrounded by Australian voices, it struck her they'd probably be the last she'd hear for eight weeks, and she was swamped by homesickness. But, for the moment at least, England was home, as she'd told the stewardess.

The years had not been kind to Rowena. As always, she wore no make-up and her skin was toughened and leathery from exposure to sub-arctic winds and tropical suns, a network of fine creases round eyes and mouth. Edward, on the other hand, looked no different from when she'd last seen him, with his crinkly red-gold hair and deepset eyes. He came forward and kissed her cheek.

"Good to see you, Janis. It's been a long time."

It was strange to hear her full name again. To Roger, and consequently to all their Australian friends, she was always "Jan." As Edward bent to greet the children, she turned to Rowena, who was proffering a dry cheek. "It's so good of you to invite us."

"Our pleasure," she replied. "I hope you've brought plenty of warm clothes; the forecast isn't good."

"We'll have to stock up here," Jan said apologetically. "In the middle of summer, there wasn't much choice at home."

She had the unreal sensation of a sleepwalker. The stress of the weeks since Roger had gone, the rushed preparations for the visit, and finally the long flight had sapped the last of her resources. She wanted to close her eyes and let someone else take control. Fortunately, Edward seemed to be doing so. He had already commandeered the trolley and was leading the way to the carpark. There, amid its bleak concrete, the dank coldness that had lurked outside closed in to envelop them. Julie shivered and pressed against her mother.

"You'll soon get warm in the car," Edward said heartily, opening the rear door for them. Naturally they were shy with each other, Jan told herself, climbing in after the children. Things would soon get easier.

Drizzling rain misted the windows and on either side of the motorway the countryside lay hidden behind a grey curtain. As they turned off at the Shillingham exit, Jan leant forward, eager for the first familiar landmarks. But to her disappointment, the changes Edward had warned her of were already in evidence. They did not, as in the past, drive through Shillingham itself, but bypassed it on a ring-road, only joining the familiar route half-way to Stonebridge. At least the imposing building of County Police Headquarters was unchanged, standing solid and four-square just short of the stone bridge that gave the district its name. She pointed it out to the children, who glanced at it as they sped by. They were very subdued, she realized, huddling against her like refugees, and Julie's lip had a disturbing quiver. Oh God, she thought for the hundredth time, had she done right, whizzing them round the world like this? Was she running away from Roger, from the prospect of a miserable Christmas, or simply from loneliness? And how long could she keep running? She hadn't stopped to wonder how the children would react to being snatched from the familiarity of warm, open-skied Australia to dank, winter-bound Britain.

She reached out a hand to both, and was rewarded by a wan smile from Julie, a more determined one from Ben.

The roar of the car's movement made conversation difficult between front and back, and she had to lean forward to catch what Edward said. Rowena sat stiffly in her seat and hadn't so much as turned her head the entire journey.

But they were almost home. Soon, Edward was driving down dear old Broad Street, with its tree-lined pavements and the towers and turrets of St. Benedict's School. Directly opposite it was the turning to Cavendish Road, and Jan leant forward eagerly. How many times she'd walked along this pavement, coming home from school, from shopping trips, from dates with Roger. And here, on the left, stood Rylands, the house about which she still dreamed so often. Yet, from the distance of fifteen years, it differed from her remembrance. She'd pictured it large and remote, standing alone with no near neighbours. In fact, it was a substantial Victorian house in a road of similar houses, neither larger nor smaller than its companions.

The front garden contained little other than a semicircular drive between the two gates. For an unfocussed moment, as Edward drew up, Jan expected her parents to come down the steps. Then he got out of the car, and with the draught of wet air reality returned, and with it a renewed sense of loss.

"Well, here we are. I hope Lily has coffee waiting."

Jan gave the children a nudge and they stumbled out onto the gravel. As Edward took their luggage from the boot, Rowena was already pushing open the front door. They followed her inside, into the welcoming warmth of the hall. At the far end, the gracious stairway rose towards the stained-glass window on the half-landing. The last time she'd come down those stairs, she'd been in her wedding dress. Now, Roger's loss was added to that of her parents. Her throat ached with unshed tears.

A small, neatly dressed woman had appeared at the back of the hall. "Oh, you're back, Mrs. Langley," she exclaimed unnecessarily. "There's a nice fire in the drawing-room."

"Thank you, Lily. This is my sister-in-law, Mrs. Coverdale, and Ben and Julie."

The woman smilingly shook hands all round. "I'll bring the coffee straight through, shall I?"

"Yes, please." Rowena was taking off her coat and hanging it in the large oak wardrobe. Jan had once hidden there, to escape a hated rice pudding. "Give me your coats," Rowena instructed, holding out her hand. "Now, I suggest we have coffee and get properly warmed through, then I'll show you your rooms and you can unpack."

Although the drawing-room had been redecorated, the furniture was still that of Jan's childhood, the deep, high-backed "Chesterfield" and matching arm-chairs, the desk which had been her father's, the grand piano with the silver-framed photograph on top. Only as she moved towards it did she notice with a jolt that the portrait had been changed. It was no longer her mother's smiling face that looked out at her, but that of a younger woman, whose make-up and hairstyle were those of the forties. Lydia Langley, her father's first wife and Edward's mother. Jan wondered what had become of her own mother's picture. She would like to have it.

"Is that Granny?" asked Julie, who had come up behind her.

"No," Jan said quietly, embarrassed to be caught studying the substitution. "That's Uncle Edward's mother."

"Why didn't you have the same mother, like me and Ben?"

"Because," Rowena said lightly from the fireplace, "your uncle's mother died. She'd been ill for a long time, and had a nurse living in the house, to look after her. And after a decent interval, your grandfather married the nurse."

Though an accurate enough summary, it lacked sensitivity, implying both that the second marriage was one of convenience, and that William Langley had married beneath him. As Jan knew, both implications were untrue. To disguise her discomfort, she walked to the French windows at the end of the room and stood staring down the long, rain-soaked garden. It must have looked as bleak in other winters, but her memory was obstinately of colour, flowers, and sunshine. Without thinking, she rested her hand on the handle and Edward, who had just come into the room, remarked, "It won't open. We have a comprehensive alarm system, and that door's sealed for the winter."

Jan turned with a smile, glad of the change of subject. "I wasn't trying to open it—I've had enough of the cold for now. But why a burglar alarm? It sounds very sinister."

"A result of one of the less admirable changes since you left. The crime rate has shot up, and burglaries are on the increase. Before we leave, we must instruct you in the intricacies of the system."

The children had flopped onto the hearth rug, and Jan moved to join them, holding out her hands to the fire. There was a tap on the door, and Lily entered with the coffee tray. That too, ornate and silver, was a familiar friend. Jan said tentatively, "I wonder if the children could have milk? They don't really care for coffee."

"Of course," Rowena said. "Bring some hot milk, would you, Lily."

"Not *hot* milk!" Julie exclaimed, before Jan could speak. "Hot milk's *disgusting!*"

Rowena raised an eyebrow. "Then by all means have it cold, and freeze your insides still further. But when I was a little girl, I drank what was provided and my opinion on it wasn't either asked or given."

Jan said quietly, "Julie often speaks without thinking, but she didn't mean to be rude, did you, Julie?"

The child, abashed by her sudden disapprobation, shook her head.

"So what do you say?" Jan prompted.

"Sorry." It was a mumble from a hung head, but it was an apology. Not sufficient, however.

"Sorry, who?" Rowena asked.

Julie looked up in bewilderment, her eyes filling with tears.

"Sorry, Aunt Rowena," Jan supplied, furious at this further chastisement.

"Sorry, Aunt Rowena," Julie repeated, and buried her face in her mother's lap. Jan stroked the tangled hair with trembling fingers. She would have a private word with her sister-in-law, she promised herself, and explain the children's insecurity and their need for temporary licence. Ben, whose own views on hot milk were mercifully forestalled by his sister's, sat glowering on the rug, his opinion of the proceedings only too apparent. And she'd *told* them to be good, Jan thought despairingly. Her own control was precarious enough; if Julie had really cried, she'd probably have howled with her.

Fortunately, the best possible distraction appeared with Lily and the milk. A sleek and creamy Siamese, tail erect and gently waving, progressed across the carpet and, ignoring the two children, took up its accustomed place before the fire.

"Careful!" Jan warned, as two delighted hands reached out towards it. "It isn't used to children."

Edward said, "If you don't rush her, she'll be quite willing to make friends."

"What's her name?" Julie asked, brushing away the last of her tears.

"Lotus. Isn't she beautiful?"

The cat turned on him its brilliant blue eyes, placidly accepting the compliment.

"What do you do with her when you're on your trips?" Jan asked.

"Board her with her breeder. Your being here will spare her that."

Coffee over, Rowena led the way upstairs. The fourth stair

from the half-landing creaked as it always had, and the worn leather cushion still lined the window-seat below the stained-glass pane. "When the sun shines through the glass, it's like sitting in a rainbow," Jan told her children.

"I've put you in the front guest-room," Rowena commented, turning to the left at the top of the stairs and opening the first door. "We've had a shower cabinet put in, which is quite useful." Lily had already brought the luggage upstairs.

"Thank you, it looks very comfortable." The room was papered in a Laura Ashley design of sprigged flowers, with matching curtains and bedspread. It was quite in keeping with the heavy mahogany suite.

"And the children are down the other end," Rowena continued, shepherding them ahead of her out of the room, "Ben in the old nursery and Julie in what was your room. I hope they'll keep them tidy, and not give Lily extra work."

"Who sleeps in all the other rooms?" asked Ben, ignoring the stricture.

"Well, there's our room, of course, and we've made the small one next to it into an *en suite* bathroom. The door to the right of the stairs is your uncle's study, and at the end of the passage are the main bathroom and lavatory."

Julie, who had run ahead to verify this last piece of information, called back excitedly, "Mummy, the lavatory's on a platform, and it's got a shiny wooden seat!"

"Where do these stairs lead to?" Ben asked, looking up the twisting narrow flight.

"The attics, of course. In the old days, the servants used to sleep there, but now they're just boxrooms used for storage."

"Where does Lily sleep?"

"At home. She comes at eight o'clock every weekday and stays until six."

"There are a lot of rooms for just two people," Ben commented, which was what Jan had been thinking. She'd known Rylands as a family home, and couldn't imagine why Edward and Rowena kept it on now; its upkeep must be considerable. Rowena was hesitating in the nursery doorway.

"I should be grateful, Janis, if both our room and the study could be considered out of bounds. Our carpet is a pale colour, easily soiled, and there are delicate ornaments in there. And, as you might remember, Edward's obsessionally neat, and not even Lily is allowed in his study."

Jan said stiffly, "We wouldn't dream of going in." Or wouldn't have, she amended mentally. The ban had probably roused the children's interest.

Rowena had the grace to look uncomfortable. "I meant during hide and seek, or whatever children play. Still, as long as that's understood, we needn't mention it again."

She left them to unpack, and the rest of the day passed in a disjointed, aimless fashion, aggravated by the malaise of jet-lag. Jan found she was tense, continually on guard for any *faux-pas* the children might make. And although no further awkwardness occurred, it was a relief when, after an early supper before Lily left, they agreed, unusually readily, to go to bed.

The three adults ate a formal meal in the dining-room. The heating had been switched on only an hour before, and the room was still chill. Jan's jaw ached from holding back yawns and it was also an effort to repress her shivers. She was thankful that Rowena suggested coffee in the drawing-room.

"Now," she began, as they settled by the fire, "what's all this about Roger?"

Edward moved uncomfortably. "Come on, darling, it's hardly our business."

"But Janis must need to confide in someone, and we are family, after all." She looked at her penetratingly as she handed her a coffee-cup.

"There's not much to tell," Jan said evasively. The last thing she wanted was to go over it now. Though she'd prepared a synopsis for just such a moment, she was too tired to remember it, and afraid any deep probing might precipitate tears.

"I presume there's someone else?" persisted Rowena.

"Would you believe the girl next door?" Jan tried to laugh. "They were new neighbours, Ron and Pam Stevens. We invited them in to meet everyone, and became quite friendly." She paused, hearing the irony in the words. "And Roger simply—lost his head. I must have been blind—I'd no idea anything was going on." She drank the hot coffee, praying it would steady her.

"And they just went off together?"

"He did apologize. He said he couldn't live without her."

Rowena snorted. "What about her husband?"

"He went to pieces. They'd only been married a year or two." Jan drew a deep breath. "That's all, really. Would you mind if we talked of something else? Tell me what you're hoping to do in Peru."

Edward, seeming relieved at the change of subject, smiled. "This trip is sheer self-indulgence. We're going to follow the Inca trail to Machu Picchu. We've always avoided it because it's so popular with tourists, but this time we're going in the rainy season, so it'll be far less crowded. And of course we won't have to worry about fresh water. From there, we'll go on to Cajabamba. We try to go back every two or three years, though it's more complicated now it's in the emergency zone."

Jan said impulsively, "I was wondering on the plane why neither Father nor Laurence Coady ever went back after '55."

Was there a tightening of the atmosphere, or had she imagined it? But something made her look up, and she was in time to catch a warning glance between husband and wife. Then Edward said easily, "Well, they'd accomplished what they set out to do, hadn't they?" Which facile explanation, offered to her in the past and accepted until now, no longer satisfied her.

"But Sir Reginald kept going back. Alone, then with Rowena, and then both of you."

"It was in his blood—he couldn't stay away. He even called his house Cajabamba."

"I remember going there for tea. And that's another thing; it seemed strange—" She broke off, smothering a yawn. "Sorry, I can hardly keep my eyes open!"

"What seemed strange?" asked Rowena, and there was a note in her voice that jerked Jan awake. However, her chain of thought had been broken.

"I can't remember!" she confessed ruefully.

Rowena was sitting forward on her chair, her clenched fist on her knee. Edward glanced at her again, and she sat back.

"I wonder if you'd excuse me?" Jan murmured. "What with the meal and the warm fire, I just can't keep awake any longer."

"Of course." Edward stood up. "Have you everything you want?"

"All I want is bed and oblivion!"

Rowena also rose to her feet. "I'll send Lily with a cup of tea at eight-thirty. Will that be all right?"

"Perfect. Goodnight, then. It's—lovely to be home."

She was aware of them both staring after her as she left the room.

CHAPTER 2

That same evening, in a flat in Bayswater, Guy Marriott, free-lance journalist, was having a drink with his girlfriend. They were sitting on a sofa, his arm across her shoulders, chatting through a mediocre television programme. Or, more accurately, he was chatting and she was trying to watch the play.

"By the way," he remarked, "I can't meet you for lunch to-morrow."

"Oh, Guy!" Momentarily diverted from the screen, the girl pouted. "But we were going to buy my Christmas present."

"Sorry, I've got to go over to Broadshire. A lead's come up on that story I'm working on."

"What story?" But she was only half-listening, and almost immediately interrupted him. "Shut up a minute, I want to listen to this bit."

Marriott laughed good-naturedly and finished his drink. Shirley had little interest beyond the cinema and TV, but she was decorative and willing, and a chap couldn't have everything. Abandoning his explanation, he got up to refill their glasses.

The next day, Jan, in company with her children, renewed her acquaintance with the town of her birth. Truth to tell, she was glad to escape from the house. Edward was out finalising his travel plans and Rowena wasn't easy company.

Also, there'd been more awkwardness involving the children. That morning Ben, on his way back from the bathroom, had momentarily lost his bearings and opened Rowena's door instead of his own. Her voice from the stairhead thundered down the corridor, stopping him on the threshold just as he realized his mistake.

"Ben! What did I say about going in there? How dare you disobey me like that?"

Her angry voice brought Jan hurrying from her own room. "For goodness' sake, Rowena! He only went one door too far. Look, darling, that one's yours."

Ben, red with fury, muttered audibly, "Who wants to go in her stupid room, anyway?" And though Rowena must have heard him, she evidently regretted over-reacting. She merely turned and went downstairs.

The other incident was more puzzling. Rowena, perhaps attempting to make amends, had, after breakfast, handed the children an enormous pile of Christmas cards to be arranged round the room. Several of them illustrated the old song "The Twelve Days of Christmas," and Ben started to sing the last verse, working his way down till he came to the ninth day. He broke off and turned to Julie.

"What's nine?"

"Nine for the Nine Bright Shiners," she supplied quickly.

Jan, smilingly about to correct her, turned sharply at a crash from behind, and saw that Rowena, suddenly white-faced, had dropped the flower vase she was carrying. After an uninterested glance over his shoulder, Ben turned back to his sister. "No, silly, that's 'Green Grow the Rushes.' I know, it's 'Nine ladies dancing'—look, here they are, on the card."

Jan slipped to her knees to pick up the broken glass. "Oh, Rowena, what a shame! Was it valuable?"

"A wedding present," Rowena said unsteadily.

"But what happened?"

"It just—slipped out of my hand and caught the edge of the table. Sheer clumsiness." But she was clearly shaken, and Jan was unconvinced.

"Julie, go and ask Lily for a cloth to mop up this water," she directed, gathering up the scattered flowers while Rowena stood motionless, watching her.

"I don't know where the kitchen is," Julie protested, with the whine Jan dreaded creeping into her voice.

"Of course you do. It's round the corner, in the back hall."

"I don't like it down there, it's all dark."

"It's a spooky house," remarked Ben unhelpfully. "Lots of dark passages and big cold rooms."

"What nonsense! Go together then—and be quick. The water's beginning to soak into the carpet."

Lily came hurrying back with them, bearing an assortment of cloths and exclaiming with concern at the shattered vase. The children, delegating responsibility, returned to the pile of cards. By this time, Rowena had regained her composure.

"Stupid of me, but so easily done. Thank you, Lily, that will do now. Will you bring another vase from the flower-room? It's all right, Janis, really," as she continued to dab at the carpet. "Such a fuss about nothing!"

And another instance of over-reaction, Jan thought, getting up and smoothing down her skirt. But what had she reacted *to?* The words of a carol? It was at that point that she decided on the expediency of exploring Broadminster. It would get the children out of Rowena's way, and in any case she was eager to see the old place again.

To her delight, they were enchanted with it, especially Monks' Walk. This lay in the heart of Old Broadminster, just across the Green from the Minster, and its roofs and chimneys clustered skywards in a glorious lack of uniformity, some crenellated, some flat, some gabled with dormer windows. Many of the old houses were white-washed, their ancient beams picked out in black paint; others were rosy in weathered brick or stone. On the ground floor, most now housed antique shops, boutiques, and coffee-houses, and their brightly lit windows were full of Christmas gifts. With fairy lights strung between the lamp-posts, the composite effect was like a scene out of fairyland. An enterprising trader was selling hot chestnuts on the corner of Queen's Road, and the children clamoured for some, burning their fingers as they attempted to shell and eat the hot nuts.

Their progress was slow, since Julie insisted they stop and gaze in each window. Over on the Green, the Salvation Army began to play carols, and the familiar tunes, albeit in very different surroundings, brought the nostalgia Jan dreaded. A man hurried past, holding tightly to the hand of a small boy, and Julie's eyes followed him. "Why doesn't Daddy love us any more?" she asked wistfully, and gave a little gasp as Ben dug her sharply in the ribs.

Jan said hurriedly, "Let's go in here; we must choose a present for your uncle and aunt."

During their stroll, she'd been aware of people staring at them. An explanation was offered by the girl in the antique shop. "My goodness, how brown you all are!" she exclaimed. "You make me look not only pale, but blue! Have you been abroad?"

"Australia," Jan confirmed. On one wall was an ornately carved mirror, and seeing their reflections in it, she was aware for the first time of the family resemblance. They were all slightly built, with fair hair bleached almost white by the Australian sun and eyes startlingly blue against their tan. No wonder they stood out among the pale English faces.

"Well, you're certainly a good advertisement! Can I help you, or do you just want to browse?"

Jan explained what they were looking for, noting that the shop sold gifts as well as antiques. She eventually chose a crystal vase for Rowena to replace the broken one, and for Edward a framed print of Broadminster in 1600. Julie was tugging at her sleeve. "Mummy, look at that funny bicycle!"

The assistant smiled at her. "It's called a penny-farthing, because the back wheel is tiny, like farthings used to be, and the front one is big, like an old penny. The shop's called after it—look!" And she held up a piece of wrapping paper covered with tiny drawings of the machine.

"Can you ride it?" Julie asked, intrigued.

The girl laughed. "I'm not allowed to try—it's quite valuable."

As they left the shop, almost colliding with a man who was passing, something familiar about him made Jan exclaim involuntarily, "Miles?"

He turned, meeting her eyes without recognition. "Good afternoon."

She said awkwardly, "It's Jan—Janis Langley-that-was. I—thought I recognized you."

"Good God!" he said, holding out his hand. "How are you? What are you doing here? I thought you were out in Canada or somewhere?"

"Australia, but we're over for Christmas."

"Well, well. Husband with you?"

"Er, no—but these are my children, Ben and Julie. Children, this is Mr. Coady, whose father was a friend of Grandpa's."

But Miles was glancing at his watch. "Well, it's good to see you after all this time. How long are you here for?"

"Oh, ages!" Jan said lightly. She hesitated. "Didn't Edward tell you we were coming?"

Miles said drily, "Edward and I don't communicate unless we have to. Look, I'm sorry to dash off, but I've an appointment in ten minutes."

"Of course—sorry to—"

"See you on Boxing Night, no doubt."

"Boxing—?" But he was already striding away, and she realized she knew no more of him than she had on the plane. Was he married? Where was he living? There'd been a time, around Edward and Rowena's wedding, when she'd fancied herself in love with Miles. She smiled wryly at the thought. But he *was* attractive, tall and broad-shouldered, still with that brooding quality he'd had as a young man.

That evening, over coffee, Jan said casually, "I met Miles Coady in town today."

"Oh, yes?" Edward's tone was neutral as he caressed the cat on his lap.

"He was surprised to see me. I thought you might have mentioned I was coming."

"We're not on the best of terms with Miles," Rowena said crisply. "He was very offensive when my father died."

"Offensive? How?"

"Oh, he came round here and started making a scene, and wouldn't leave when we asked him. It was all very unpleasant."

"Surely he was fond of your father?"

"It's my mother he's fond of, and she of him, unfortunately. But it goes back a long way."

"Then I don't see—"

"Please, Janis, I'd rather not say any more."

After a moment Jan murmured, "He said he'd see me on Boxing Night. I didn't know what he meant."

"We always have a party."

"And you've invited Miles?"

"Season of good will," Edward said facetiously, and Rowena threw him a disparaging glance.

"Because of Mother. It'll be hard enough for her this Christmas, the first without Father. We couldn't deprive her of Miles as well."

Jan was silent. She remembered vaguely that Lady Peel had looked after Miles as a child, but she'd never known why, and this hardly seemed the time to ask.

"And what did you think of Broadminster?" Edward inquired, adroitly leading her off the subject. "Has it changed much?"

"Not Monks' Walk, but that's hardly changed in three hundred years, let alone fifteen!"

"It's geared for tourists, though," Rowena put in. "You can't move for them in the season. Still, there are some interesting boutiques. I bought a very smart wedding outfit there last summer."

"We went in one of the antique shops, and Julie was intrigued with a penny-farthing they had on display."

"Oh, Pennyfarthings—yes. They had a murder there a year or two ago."

"A *murder?*" Jan stared at her aghast. "In the shop?"

"The flat above, I believe, but the staff were involved. All very gory and unpleasant."

"But who, and why?"

"I don't remember the details. But as Edward said, times have changed, even if it's not all that apparent on the surface. Everything seems more violent now, even in sleepy old Broadminster."

Jan shuddered, her pleasant memory of the shopping trip spoiled. The stain of violence was far-spreading, contaminating long after the initial act had been expunged.

Edward gave a short laugh. "Poor Janis! You'll be regretting having come! But surely you have crime down in Oz too?"

"Yes—yes, of course." But it hadn't touched her as closely as this nebulous encroachment in the town she still thought of as home.

Christmas, anticipated either with dread or excitement for so long, came in the end with a rush. On Christmas Eve, Lady Peel arrived to spend the holiday at Rylands. She was a charming woman, grey-haired, erect, and always impeccably dressed. Jan was pleased to meet her again, recalling her mother's description of Lady Peel as "a gentlewoman." Her manner with the children immediately endeared her to them, since, unlike her daughter, she treated them with grave politeness, listening carefully to what they had to say. It was a shame, Jan thought, that she'd no grandchildren.

Later that evening, Jan sat on the bedroom floor, as she did every year, filling the children's stockings. In the past, Roger had always been with her, wrapping the small gifts in tissue paper and passing them to her to stuff into the long legs. What was he doing now? she wondered, pushing the oddly shaped packages down to the toe. Surfing on the beach? Having a barbecue? She hadn't told him they were coming away, chiefly because she knew he'd try to dissuade her. She'd intended to drop him a line as soon as they arrived, but in the build-up to Christmas he wouldn't in any case have received it before the holiday. She promised herself she'd write as soon as it was over.

The strains of "Away in a Manger" came from beneath her window, followed almost immediately by the sound of the door-bell. Despite being twelve thousand miles from Roger and in the bosom of her family, Jan would be glad when the next few days were over.

The next morning dawned still and crisp with frost, a relief after the strong gales of the last few days. It was, Jan reflected, the next best thing to a white Christmas.

It was as they were getting ready for church that Roger phoned. With dry mouth and clattering heart, she went down to take the call. The phone was in the hall, and though doors were discreetly closed, she knew the children were listening on the landing. She said carefully, "Hello?"

"Jan!" He sounded almost at her side. "What the hell are you doing over there?"

"Merry Christmas, Roger," she said steadily. "Would you like to speak to the children?"

"I'd like to speak to you first. Why didn't you tell me you were going?"

"Can't you guess?"

"But I've got all your presents. I called at the house with them last night."

"I was going to write—"

"Hell, you knew I'd want to see you all over the holiday."

"Exactly," she said.

There was a pause. Then he said flatly, "So it was just to thwart me. Is that what you're saying?"

"Not really. I—needed some moral support, and Edward wrote inviting us."

"How long are you staying?"

"Till the children go back to school."

"Another six weeks? I won't see you for six weeks?"

She said tightly, "If you'd wanted to see us—" and broke off.

"Yes," he said, and his voice was tired, "I get your point. But I need to talk to you, Jan. There's been no contact between us since I left—that's not the way I wanted it." He paused, waiting for her comment, but she was incapable of making one. She heard him sigh. "OK, I appreciate this is neither the time nor place— Are the kids there, then?"

She looked up and, as she'd expected, saw them hanging over the banister. She nodded to them, thinking that, as in the past when Roger phoned, they'd come hurtling downstairs, fighting to be first to reach the phone. Now, however, they hesitated, and she put a hand over the mouthpiece. "Hurry up—it's Daddy. Heavens knows what this call is costing."

They came down slowly, and Ben took the receiver. "Hello, Dad." He stood listening gravely to his father's voice, giving monosyllabic answers to a series of questions. After two or three minutes, he silently handed the phone to Julie. She took it, said tremulously, "I miss you, Daddy," and burst into tears. Jan retrieved the instrument, her other arm pressing the child against her.

"I'm sorry, Roger. Perhaps this isn't such a good idea."

"But I had to ring, Jan. Damn it, you're still my family."

She said unsteadily, "We must go. It's time for church, and Lady Peel's waiting. Goodbye, and—happy Christmas." And, sadly, she put down the phone.

On their return from church, Edward and Rowena, who had not accompanied them, were waiting in the drawing-room. A tinsel tree had been set up near the window, and beneath it was a pile of gaily coloured packages. Jan, trying to put Roger's phone-call out of her mind, brought down her own parcels, and soon everyone was exclaiming over their presents. Edward, she was glad to note, seemed genuinely pleased with the seventeenth-century print. Rowena had given him, as well as a cashmere sweater, a luxurious wallet bearing his initials in gold.

"Just what I need," he said, kissing her, and turned to Jan. "My last one was stolen a few weeks ago, and I hadn't got round to replacing it."

"I hope there wasn't much in it," Jan said.

Her half-brother shrugged. "Enough. Fifty quid or so, and all my credit cards. It was they that caused the most bother. Pinched from the squash club, if you please, along with several others. As I said, Janis, you can't trust anyone these days."

"And as *I* said," Rowena reminded him severely, "you should have taken your valuables into the court with you. Oh, Janis— how kind! What a pretty vase! Thank you so much."

Julie, having torn open all the parcels addressed to her, was playing with the cat, laughing as it pounced on the crumpled balls of wrapping paper and patted them adroitly under a chair. "What time are we eating?" she asked as, tiring of the game, the animal sat down and started to wash itself.

"It's ready any time," Rowena said. "We're not having the turkey till this evening."

"This *evening?*" Ben repeated, and Julie added anxiously, "We can stay up for it, can't we?"

"Of course," Rowena said smoothly. "And as I was saying, there's salmon and salad in the dining-room."

"But we *always* have the turkey at lunch-time," Ben said rebelliously. "Everyone does—that's the proper time for it. At home, we eat on the verandah, and Dad puts on a paper hat to carve, and we're not allowed to swim for two hours after we've finished."

"If you ask me," Rowena countered, "it's the height of lunacy to eat an enormous lunch in temperatures like that. How you can—"

"It isn't lunacy at all!" Ben flared. "And Australia's a lot better than your beastly cold, wet country!"

"Ben!" Jan murmured helplessly.

"*My* country?" Rowena raised her eyebrows. "My dear child, don't forget you're British too, despite that distressing Australian twang."

Ben stared at her for a moment, his face suffused with colour. Then he turned and hurled himself out of the room. Jan, fighting down her instinct to follow him, turned instead to her hostess. "I'm sorry, Rowena." It seemed she was always apologizing for the children.

"He's very insolent, isn't he?" Rowena remarked icily. "A good smacking wouldn't go amiss, in my opinion."

"He's missing his father, dear," Lady Peel put in peaceably. "We must make allowances."

"It doesn't excuse rudeness, Mother. However, I refuse to let it spoil my Christmas. And as I was saying, lunch is ready as soon as you are."

As the others started to move towards the dining-room, Lady

Peel patted Jan's hand. "Don't worry, my dear. Rowena wasn't very tactful, but she's unused to children. And in Ben's defence, I think he felt it was an oblique criticism of his father."

"But when Roger phoned, Ben would hardly speak to him," Jan said shakily.

"Wasn't that out of loyalty to you?"

Jan stared at her. "You mean if I'd left them to it, not stood listening—? I never thought of that." Her eyes filled. "Poor Roger, he must have felt awful. I didn't realize it was my fault."

Lady Peel said quietly, "You're missing him too, aren't you, despite putting a brave face on it. I understand only too well— I've lost my husband as well, you know." And Jan, her control precarious, could only squeeze her hand in reply.

Ben appeared at lunch somewhat chastened, but his outburst wasn't referred to again and gradually his normal exuberance returned. However, that night, having escaped from the soporific atmosphere in the drawing-room, Jan, on her way to bed, heard muffled sobbing coming from his room. She pushed the door open and went in, sitting on his bed and smoothing the damp hair off his forehead. And, as he had as a small child, he came up into her arms, sobbing against her chest. Jan sat cradling him in silence until his breathing quietened, and with a shaky and embarrassed smile, he lay back again. She bent and kissed him and, still without a word passing between them—for what was there to say?—she quietly went out again.

The following afternoon, presumably to offer escape from the fatuous holiday programmes, BBC2 screened a recorded interview with Edward on his proposed trip to Peru. He and Rowena, setting out glasses and drinks for the evening's party, professed no interest, but Jan sat down with Lady Peel and the children to watch it. There were several clips of film taken on previous trips, and the children were enthralled as their fairy-tale land came alive.

"Of course, Mr. Langley, it was your father who discovered

the lost city of Cajabamba, back in the fifties. Are you hoping to come across another major Inca ruin?"

Edward shrugged. "Peru's been pretty exhaustively covered over the last few decades. Still, with all that virtually impenetrable jungle, there's always a chance. We explorers are an optimistic bunch."

"One last question, then. Having seen some of Peru's most priceless treasures, which do you consider the most valuable?"

Edward hesitated, his face large in close-up, and for a moment Jan fancied she saw wariness in his eyes. Then he laughed. "Without doubt, the potato! That's where it originated, and I assure you the annual world harvest is many times more valuable than all the treasures stolen by the Spanish."

Across the room, Edward had paused to watch the final exchange, and smiled at his mother-in-law's rueful laugh.

Jan turned to him. "That was dodging the issue, wasn't it? Which *treasure* is the most valuable?"

His eyes held hers for a moment, then he shrugged. "Impossible to answer. The most priceless were melted down, as you know. At Cajamarca alone, over eleven tons of gold went into the furnaces—vases, figures, jewellery—God knows what."

Jan smiled, abandoning her questions. "All this talk of Peru is making me restless. For two pins I'd come with you on Monday!"

Jan did not enjoy that evening. Rowena had primed her guests well, and not one, when introduced, made any mention of Roger or her solitary state. Nevertheless, she was permanently braced to answer such questions, and her face ached from the obligatory smile. Even Miles, the only guest whom she knew, made little attempt to talk to her. He took his place at Lady Peel's side, and only when the old lady called Jan across did he direct one or two comments to her. He seemed on edge, but that might have been his usual manner, especially in a house where he knew he wasn't welcome.

All in all, the atmosphere of determined gaiety and bonhomie was too much for Jan, and as early as she could, she pleaded a headache and escaped to bed. At last, she thought thankfully, Christmas was over, and after Monday she and the children would have the house to themselves. Edward and Rowena had been kind in their way, but the continual watching that the children didn't annoy them had been a strain, and she acknowledged guiltily that she'd be glad to see them off.

At the back of the cupboard were a few overlooked scraps of newspaper and a painted football. But the tramp-like figure had disappeared.

CHAPTER 3

Of all Mondays in the year, Detective Chief Inspector Webb thought gloomily, that after the Christmas and New Year break was undoubtedly the worst. Admittedly, Shillingham CID had not been favoured with the extended holiday enjoyed by the rest of the country, but the feeling of anticlimax was nevertheless strong.

Nor was it only post-holiday lethargy that made him jaded. Alan Crombie had departed on a three-month course at Bramshill, and in his absence DI Stanley Bates from "C" Division was sitting in for him. Sitting in, what was more, in Webb's own office. And Stanley Bates, while no doubt a competent enough police officer, was not someone in whose company Webb took any pleasure.

He glanced across the room, his eyes moving sourly over the man at Crombie's desk. The dark hair, parted down the centre, was plastered against his head—whether by grease or haircream Webb had refrained from ascertaining, but he looked like a fugitive from the thirties. He also had a long nose, thin lips, and a habit of nodding vigorously while being addressed, giving the impression that he already knew what he was being told and was hurrying the speaker along. Worst of all—the final straw, in fact, to Webb's way of thinking—he was teetotal. Who the hell was he going to moan to over a pint in the Brown Bear for the next three months?

Webb sighed deeply. He'd the feeling he was going to miss Alan Crombie every bit as much as his wife did. Dispiritedly, he pulled a pile of papers towards him, running a jaundiced eye over the list of suspicious deaths which had taken place over the weekend. Ken Jackson was attending a post mortem at the mo-

ment—chap found under a tree at the back of a layby. The tree
had blown down in the pre-Christmas gales, and because of the
long holiday, the council workmen had only gone along this
morning to remove it. And found more than they bargained for.

Webb's attention wandered again. Hannah would be back this
evening, thank God. She'd been spending New Year with her
aunt in Oxford, and since he himself went to his sister's for
Christmas, he hadn't seen her for nearly two weeks. Perhaps
they could—

The phone on his desk shrilled, making him jump. "Webb."

"Ken here, guv. I'm at the mortuary."

"Yes?"

"We've found something a bit fishy. Stapleton's not happy, so
I've asked him to hold it till you get here."

"Right, I'm on my way." He was coming to his feet as he
spoke, and Bates looked up from his desk.

"Anything I can do, skipper?"

"Not a thing, thanks. If anyone wants me, I'm at the morgue."

That was another thing about Bates, Webb reflected as he ran
down the stairs, his persistent use of the word "skipper" or
"skip" instead of the familiar "governor." Nothing wrong with
it, but for some reason it grated. Impatiently, he pushed the
man and his idiosyncrasies from his mind.

The wind, which had dropped over the last week or so, was
rising again, blowing its cold breath down the back of his collar
as he hurried, head down, to the General Hospital next to the
police station. A group of young nurses ahead of him giggled
and shrieked as their capes billowed out about them, and he
moved to one side as an ambulance, siren sounding, turned into
the gateway and drove up to the main entrance. In the midst of
life—he thought morosely.

Jackson was waiting for him outside the post mortem room.
"Several odd things on this one, guv. I'll let Stapleton tell you
his side, and fill in the details later."

They went together into the bleak, sterile room, where
gowned men were gathered round the slab. The stench of de-
composing flesh mingling with strong disinfectant seared the

back of Webb's throat. It was the familiar smell of death. He nodded to the SOCOs and photographer, and glanced as briefly as possible at the body on the slab. It was a man, with reddish fair hair growing low on his forehead. He turned to the pathologist.

"Trouble, Dr. Stapleton?"

"Queries, Chief Inspector. The deceased was found under a tree, on the layby just short of Chedbury."

"Yes?"

"I can now inform you that the tree was in no way responsible for his death."

"He was already dead when it fell?"

"That is my assumption, yes." Pedantic bastard, thought Webb impatiently. Why doesn't he get to the point? "I also noted, when I was called to the scene, that there were no ditches or even puddles in the immediate vicinity."

Webb frowned. "Puddles?"

"Puddles," repeated Stapleton, and allowed himself a brief, dramatic pause. "The cause of death, Chief Inspector, was drowning."

Two hours later, Webb was back in his office with Sergeant Jackson. "Right, Ken, let's go over it again. According to papers found on the body, he appears to be Edward Langley, of Rylands, Cavendish Road, Broadminster."

"Edward Langley?" Bates looked up from his desk. "Not the explorer, skip?"

Webb raised an eyebrow. "Explorer?"

"Yes, he was on TV over Christmas. About to set off for Peru."

"Well, it looks as though he never got there," Webb said heavily. "Anyway, by Christmas he was already under that tree."

"It could have been a recording," Jackson offered. "Bound to be, when you think of it."

"Let's leave that for the moment. I want to recap on the clothes. Forget I saw them, Ken, and tell me how they struck you."

"If he's a well-known bloke, it's even stranger, isn't it, him being dressed like that?"

"A description of his clothes, Ken."

"Old tweed jacket, shabby flannels, and a tatty jumper."

"Go on."

"That's it, guv, isn't it? No vest, underpants, shoes, or socks. It makes you cold, just thinking of it!"

"He was past worrying about that. Go on about the jacket."

"Well, it had these sequins on the lapel."

"Sequins?" interrupted Bates, and catching Webb's frown, subsided with a muttered apology. But Jackson was answering him.

"That's right—green ones, sewn on with big stitches. And in the pocket was the wallet with fifty quid in it, and credit cards in the name of Edward Langley. Oh, and there was something else. His right arm was tightly bandaged, but there was no sign of any injury."

Webb slammed his hand on his desk. "It doesn't make sense, Ken. Any of it. If he was a famous man, which ties in with the wallet, what the hell was he doing dressed like a tramp?"

"Perhaps his own clothes were wet from the drowning, so the killer dressed him in these."

"Which he just happened to have by him? And why on earth bother? To stop him catching a chill?" Webb's voice was heavy with sarcasm. "Another point: most killers try to disguise their victim's identity, to give themselves a head start. They don't transfer his wallet from his own clothes to whatever they decide to dress him in, without even removing the money, at that. And what the *hell* is the meaning of those sequins? They belong on "Come Dancing" dresses, not a shabby sports jacket." He sighed. "Well, we'll have to get on to the relatives, to identify him positively." He looked across at Bates.

"Fancy a trip to Broadminster, Stan?"

"Yes, of course, skip."

"Take Sally Pierce with you. I'll get on to DCI Horn as a matter of courtesy, but since he was found on our patch, I reckon he's our pigeon. Tact, understanding, and sympathy, that's all that's required. Don't for God's sake give them any details, whatever they ask."

Bates said stiffly, "I've informed relatives before, Chief Inspector."

"Just reminding you. I want no hint of suspicious circumstances until they get here." Webb glanced out of the window. "It's too dark to go out to the scene now, Ken. We'll have to wait till morning. In the meantime, we can make a start on the preliminary report."

It had been quite a pleasant day. In the morning, Jan had bought the children some warm clothes in the January sales. They had lunched at a Wimpey Bar, then gone to the local pantomime, *Humpty Dumpty.* Consequently, she was later than usual preparing supper, and tired herself now, was looking forward to a relaxing evening after the children were in bed. She had just taken the dish from the oven when the doorbell sounded through the house.

Jan frowned, glancing at the kitchen clock. It was seven-fifteen, an odd time for callers. Remembering Edward's comments on the rise of crime, she felt a quiver of apprehension. She and the children were, after all, alone in the house. At the front door she paused, calling, "Who is it?"

"Shillingham police, ma'am. CID."

Was this the latest criminal ploy? "Can I see your identification?"

The flap of the letterbox lifted and a warrant card came through. She glanced at it briefly and pulled the door open, one anxiety giving way to another. A man and woman stood on the step.

"What is it? What's happened?"

"Mrs. Langley?"

"No, I'm afraid she's away. I'm her sister-in-law, Janis Coverdale."

"If we could have a word, ma'am?"

Ben's face came round the library door. Since they'd been alone, they'd taken to using the smaller, warmer room at the front of the house rather than the large and bleak drawing-room.

"Who is it, Mum?"

"Some friends of Uncle's," she said quickly. "Go through to the kitchen, and you can be having your supper while I speak to them."

The two police officers came into the house, and at her gesture, went to wait in the library while she served the meal. *Shillingham* police? she thought in confusion. What on earth could they want? With a final glance at the children happily tucking into their supper at the kitchen table, she hurried back to her visitors, her heart beating uncomfortably. "Now—what is it?" she asked.

"Perhaps you'd like to sit down, ma'am." It was the man who'd done all the talking—an odd-looking man with a pale face, whose hair seemed to be painted on his head. The woman, young and red-haired, looked gravely sympathetic, which alarmed Jan still further. *Roger?* Had something happened to Roger?

She said sharply, "It's not my husband, is it?"

The woman said gently, "This is Detective Inspector Bates and I'm Constable Pierce. You say you're Mrs. Coverdale?"

Jan nodded, swallowing hard.

"And Mrs. Langley's your sister-in-law?"

"Yes, she's married to my half-brother."

The two exchanged glances. Bates said, "Have you any idea where your brother is, Mrs. Coverdale?"

Her mind still on Roger, she stared at him blankly.

"Do you know—" he began again.

"Yes—I'm sorry. He's in Peru. He and his wife flew out last week."

Again the exchange of looks, puzzled this time. "Did you see him off at the airport?"

"No."

"Then you don't know for certain that he left?"

"Of course I know." She stopped. "What is this? What are you trying to say?"

"We're afraid he may have met with an accident, Mrs. Coverdale. In the absence of his wife, we'd be grateful if you'd come with us and—confirm his identity."

"You mean he's *dead?*" Her eyes were wide with horror.

Sally Pierce said quickly, "Someone is."

"But why should you think it's Edward?"

"He had papers in his pocket."

"Oh God," Jan whispered. *Had* Edward and Rowena really left for Peru? And if Edward had had an accident, where was Rowena? She moistened her lips. "You want me to come now?"

She'd have to take the children with her; the only person she could have left them with was Lady Peel, and she was away for a few days. But it was adult support she was in need of. Miles?

"Could I bring a friend with me?" she asked the detectives.

"An excellent idea."

Jan scrabbled frantically through the telephone directory, but when she'd found and dialled Miles's number, it was answered by a machine. She left a brief, incoherent message, and rang off. There was to be no help from that quarter.

The journey to Shillingham was a nightmare. The children, alarmed by events they didn't understand, kept plying her with questions, which the police seemed unwilling to help her answer. Above all, she was dreading the ordeal ahead. In a wave of retrospective affection, she conjured up her half-brother and his wife in her mind: Edward with his crinkly hair and deepset eyes, Rowena, flat-chested and plummy-voiced, habitually in tweed skirt and ankle socks. Oh, please God, don't let it be Edward lying there!

But even if it wasn't, she would at least have to look at the body, and she'd never seen anyone dead before. And they hadn't told her how he'd died; if it were a road accident, he might be horribly disfigured. Oh God, Roger, I wish you were here!

Determinedly she closed her mind to the possibilities, looking instead out of the window. The car was roaring along the familiar road, carving itself a tunnel of light from the darkness. On their left this time, Police Headquarters stood impassive, its windows a blaze of light. Ironic she should have pointed it out before; little had she thought she'd be having dealings with them herself.

Shillingham was still festooned with Christmas lights. How long ago it seemed, Jan thought with a shiver, since they were gathered round the tree exchanging presents. She frowned, some elusive memory hovering just beyond recall, something that might explain—

"Here we are," Sally Pierce said bracingly, as the police car turned into Carrington Street. It drew up outside the General Hospital, and Sally added, "Mr. Webb would like to see you afterwards, Mrs. Coverdale. I'll take the children straight up to his office."

Jan nodded. "Thank you." Her stomach knotted with apprehension, she got out of the car, shivering, and watched as, with the woman constable now in the driving-seat and Julie's anxious face pressed to the back window, the car moved on to the police station next door. Inspector Bates had taken her arm. No doubt he meant to support her, but she wondered if he thought she'd run away. "This way, ma'am," he said.

Fifteen minutes later, Jan, pale and trembling, was gratefully sipping tea in Webb's office. The children had gone to the canteen with Constable Pierce, and Inspector Bates was back at his desk.

"And you're sure," the Chief Inspector was saying, "that the man is not your brother?"

"Absolutely," Jan said thankfully. "I've never seen him before."

"Is there any resemblance between them?"

"Yes, he'd quite a look of Edward." She looked up, meeting Webb's eyes. They were kind at the moment, but something about them, together with the set of his mouth, made her glad she wasn't meeting him as a felon. "Someone said he'd some papers on him?"

Webb pushed a photograph towards her. It was of a pigskin

wallet with the initials EWL stamped in gold. "That was in his pocket, complete with credit cards in your brother's name and fifty pounds in notes."

Jan stared at it, and the elusive memory clicked into focus. Rowena giving Edward a new wallet, because—

"It was stolen," she said.

Webb straightened. "When was that?"

"A few weeks ago, he said. From the changing room at the squash club."

"Was the theft reported?"

"I should think so. Several others were taken at the same time."

Webb glanced at Bates. "Check with Broadminster, would you, Inspector? Use the phone in the outer office."

Bates nodded and left the room, passing Sergeant Jackson in the doorway. Webb introduced him to Jan. "The deceased is not Edward Langley," he told Jackson shortly, "so we're back to square one."

Jan said tentatively, "How did he die?"

"Drowned, then dumped in a layby outside town."

"Drowned?" She looked at him in bewilderment, but he didn't elaborate.

"That's right. And as luck would have it, a tree blew down in the gales before Christmas, hiding him from view: which accounts for the delay in finding him."

"And he had my brother's wallet. Perhaps it was he who stole it."

"Perhaps, but it's more complicated than that. There are other incongruities we needn't bother you with."

"Like what?"

"Well, he was dressed in shabby clothes—I mean *really* shabby, like a tramp—and for some reason, green sequins had been sewn on his jacket. Then there was a bandage on his arm, but no apparent reason for it. The pathologist says it was put on after death."

"A very tight bandage," Jackson added. "They had to cut it off. Almost like a mummy, Dr. Stapleton said."

"That's funny!" Jan exclaimed involuntarily.

"What is?"

"The mention of a mummy. With my brother being an explorer, I mean."

Webb pursed his lips, staring at her thoughtfully. "Surely his area's South America, not Egypt."

"But the Incas had mummies too. They were sometimes wrapped, but more often dressed in their own clothes." Webb's eyes were boring into hers, slate-grey and unreadable. She added falteringly, "It was the cold, dry air, you see. They didn't need embalming."

"That's extremely interesting, Mrs. Coverdale," he said slowly. "It opens up several possibilities."

Jan's eyes widened. "You think the bandage was *intended* to make us think of mummies? And there's the wallet, too." She shuddered. "I was so relieved it wasn't Edward, but it's not that simple, is it? In some horrible way he's still involved—almost as though we were *supposed* to think it was him. But what could be the point? As soon as relatives arrived, the mistake would be discovered."

Webb drew the photograph back, frowning down at it. "That, Mrs. Coverdale, is what we'll have to find out. In the meantime, I'm sorry to have subjected you to all this."

Inspector Bates came back into the room. "The theft of the wallets was reported on the first of November, skip. Four were taken in all, but the odd thing is, the other three were returned soon afterwards, all with their contents intact. At Court Lane they'd written it off as a practical joke, and were expecting Mr. Langley's to turn up as well."

"And so it has," Webb said grimly. "Thanks, Inspector. Now, perhaps you and WDC Pierce will run Mrs. Coverdale home."

As the door closed behind them, Webb sighed, rubbing a hand across his face. "So there we are, Ken. Far from clearing things up, it's more incomprehensible than ever. And we don't even know who we've got down there. We'll have to check Missing Persons, but first let's jot down some random thoughts. Apart from the basics of establishing identity, we want to know

1) if the deceased was wearing his own clothes, and if he sewed on those sequins himself. Not to mention why. 2) If they *were* his clothes, he must have been down-and-out, so why the hell, having stolen the wallets, did he return three intact and not spend the fifty quid in Langley's? He must have hung on to it for seven weeks or more."

"If it was him that stole the wallets," Jackson interrupted. "I was thinking, guv, he couldn't have got into the squash club undetected, dressed like that."

"True, Ken, he couldn't. So if *he* didn't take them, we have to assume the killer did. Any thoughts on that?"

"Seems a funny idea, pinching wallets when you don't need the money. I mean, what's the point?"

Webb ran his eye down the list of contents. "There was nothing else in this one except credit cards, and he left those, too. As you say, it doesn't make sense."

"And it's odd, what Mrs. Coverdale said about the mummy. You reckon we were really supposed to work all that out from the bandage?"

Webb shrugged. "Seems pretty far-fetched. I'd never connected mummies with South America, so it meant damn-all to me."

"But if it *was* intentional, I suppose he knew someone connected with the Langleys would get the message."

"And that's another big question-mark. Why was he so anxious to make us think we'd got Edward Langley?"

Jackson said slowly, "He didn't try that hard, did he? OK, so there was the wallet and the bandage, but why the old clothes? Langley wouldn't have been seen dead in them." He paused, realized what he'd said, and grinned sheepishly.

Webb said heavily, "Well, that's what we *don't* know. Let's cheer ourselves up by listing what we do. Not that there's much. According to Doc Stapleton, the water in the lungs was tap water, but not soapy—there were no bubbles. Which means our man wasn't taking a bath voluntarily. The bang on the back of his head would have knocked him out, then he must have been lugged to a bathroom somewhere, tipped into the bath, and cold-bloodedly drowned.

"Which, on reflection, makes it unlikely those were his own clothes. If he was dumped fully dressed in the bath, the killer wouldn't fancy carrying a dripping corpse out to the car and leaving a trail of water behind him. But why not dump him starkers? Why go to all the trouble of dressing him again? And where did the clothes come from? The killer would hardly be daft enough to use his own." He made an impatient movement. "Let's leave the question-marks for the moment. Get the Control room to send a 'Misper' message to all Forces. You've got his general description. We might get a lead from that."

And they did. One Guy Marriott of Bayswater, London, age thirty-six, six foot two, red-blond hair, blue eyes, was known to have intended visiting Broadshire on December 18 and had not been seen since. His girlfriend reported him missing at once, but the police had allowed two weeks before initiating inquiries, in case it had simply been a lovers' tiff. Webb pulled his phone towards him, dialled, and spoke briefly into it.

"OK, Ken, they'll bring his girlfriend over in the morning. Thank God it's been cold and dry the last fortnight. That and the shelter of the tree slowed down putrefaction, for which we can all be grateful." He looked at his watch. "Nearly nine o'clock. We need our wits about us on this one, and today's gone on long enough. Of all the Mondays I've ever known, this one takes the biscuit! First thing in the morning we'll go out and look at the scene. We'll have time before they arrive from London, and it might give us something. In the meantime, let's call it a day."

CHAPTER 4

Jan could hear the phone ringing as she fought with rubbery fingers to fit the key in the lock.

"Answer it for me, Ben," she said breathlessly, as they all stepped inside. "But for heaven's sake don't open any doors till I've turned off the alarm."

The police car, having waited till they were safely in the house, moved away.

"It's Miles Coady," Ben repeated, as she emerged from the meter cupboard where the alarm was located. "Is it all right to go in the library now?"

"Just for five minutes, then bed." She took the phone. "Hello, Miles."

"Janis! I got your message on the answer-phone and I've been trying to get you ever since. Wherever have you been?"

She leaned wearily against the wall. "I'm sorry, I shouldn't have bothered you, but I thought if—"

"What's happened?"

"I had to go to Shillingham to identify a body they thought was Edward's." She heard her voice crack.

"You *what?*" Then, without giving her time to repeat it, he said quickly, "It *wasn't* Edward, was it?"

"No." The single word sounded inadequate, but she couldn't think what to add.

"Are you all right? You sound very shaky."

"It wasn't a very pleasant experience."

"Look—would you like me to come round for an hour or so? We could discuss it, and perhaps you'd feel better."

"Oh, Miles, would you?" She felt weak with relief.

"No problem. In half an hour's time?"

"That would be fine. I've just got to settle the children."

It was an effort to put the phone down and go through to the library. She was shaking both with cold and reaction, and her legs felt unsteady. They'd switched on the television, but only from habit. The news was of no interest to them, and they turned as she came in.

"Upstairs, both of you. Mr. Coady's coming round, and I don't want a squeak out of either of you. I'll bring up some cocoa and a biscuit in five minutes, so don't brush your teeth yet."

Without a murmur, they trooped past her and started up the stairs. The passage leading to the kitchen was dim, the light from the front hall not extending far round the corner. Jan shuddered, feeling along the wall for a switch but unable to find one, and reached the kitchen door with a sense of relief. The children's supper plates were still on the table, their chairs pushed back as they'd hurried to get ready for the car journey. She opened the oven, glanced at her own dried-up supper, and tipped it in the bin.

What an interminable day! she reflected, taking milk from the fridge. She thought back to that afternoon at the pantomime, the long-legged Principal Boy and the Dame in her striped petticoats. She'd had no inkling, then, that she was about to be touched by murder.

Her hand jerked, tipping the pan and sending the frothing milk up the side of it. Murder? her brain repeated incredulously, the word registering itself for the first time. Though she'd known the man's death wasn't natural, subconsciously she'd refused to follow it through. Yet he'd been *murdered*, that man who looked like Edward, and even more frighteningly, he'd had Edward's wallet in his pocket. Did that mean Edward himself was known to the killer?

The milk rose in a curling white foam and she snatched up the pan and emptied it into the mugs on the table. Thank God Miles was coming. She badly needed to talk through her fears.

It was good of him to have phoned back. As she carried the mugs upstairs, she tried to recall the message she'd left him.

Whatever it was, she must have sounded distraught enough for him to make repeated attempts to contact her. Considering that he'd barely acknowledged her existence on Boxing Night, she was duly grateful.

The children, unaware of the implications of their unexpected night-ride, drank their cocoa while she told them the story of Atahualpa's ransom. Bloodthirsty it might be, but familiarity had reduced it to the safe, acceptable horror of a fairy-tale.

"A roomful of gold," Julie repeated dreamily, with echoes of Rumpelstiltskin. They finished their cocoa, brushed their teeth, and were saying their prayers when the doorbell announced Miles's arrival. Jan was about to bundle them into bed, when Julie sank back to her knees, eyes squeezed tight. "P.S.," she added, somewhat irreverently. "Please keep Uncle and Auntie safe, and don't let the Spaniards catch them!"

Jan, steering her daughter into bed, realized that a modern history lesson was well overdue.

The sight of Miles, tall and dark on the front step, brought a wave of relief. She was not, after all, totally alone.

"It is good of you to come," she greeted him.

He glanced briefly at her as he stepped inside. "You sounded in need of company, and I presume there's no one else."

"It's all been so unnerving."

He removed his coat and dropped it over a chair. "Any alcohol in the house?"

"I think so—in the dining-room sideboard."

"I'll get it. Go and sit down—you'll feel better with a drink inside you."

Obediently she went to the library. It occurred to her that she hadn't eaten since lunchtime, but the thought of food made her nauseous. She knelt down and poked the fire into new life, throwing on some logs from the wicker basket on the hearth. Miles came in behind her and she heard the clink of glasses. He handed her one and sat down opposite her, his dark, brooding eyes on her face.

"Now," he said, "what the hell's this all about?"

Carefully, sipping the drink as she went along, she told him what had happened, and the more she recounted, the more unbelievable it seemed.

Miles listened intently, his disconcerting eyes on her face.

"Good God!" he said softly, when she came to an end. "No wonder you're shaken. What an experience."

"I'd never seen anyone dead before."

After a moment he said, "Since the police thought it was Edward till you disabused them, I presume they've no other ideas?"

"I suppose not. Apparently he was dressed like a tramp."

"With Edward's wallet in his pocket. I knew it had been stolen —mine was taken at the same time, but I got it back later, all intact. Was anything taken from Edward's, did you gather?"

"I don't think so. The police said there was fifty pounds in it, which was the sum Edward mentioned at Christmas. There were a couple of other things, too. He had a bandage tightly wrapped round his arm which, according to the pathologist, had been put on after death."

Miles frowned. "What the hell for?"

Jan shrugged helplessly. "And his jacket had sequins on it."

"Oh, come on!"

"That's what they said. Really."

"You mean he was dressed as a clown, or something?"

"No, just—a few sequins, that's all."

"Well, I suppose it takes all sorts. You said he'd been drowned. Were there any details?"

Jan shivered. "I didn't ask. Miles, what frightens me is that Edward seems to be implicated. Apart from the wallet, the man even had a look of him."

"Pure coincidence. And there'll be a logical explanation for everything else, too."

"According to the police, he'd been there some time—since before Christmas, they said."

"Then why hadn't he been found?"

"Because a tree'd blown down and covered him. Some men went to move it this morning, and that's when he was discovered."

"If he'd been found straight away," Miles said thoughtfully, "Edward would have been here and you wouldn't have had to go through this. The killer must have been chewing his fingernails, waiting for the story to break. He couldn't have known about the tree."

"Unless he went back to look."

Miles's mouth twisted. "Revisiting the scene of crime? I doubt if he'd risk it. He's probably miles away by now."

"I hope so," Jan said with a shiver.

He frowned. "You're not really worried, are you? This has nothing whatever to do with you."

"I wish he hadn't had Edward's wallet, that's all."

"It could have been anyone's."

Jan was silent. She was reluctant to tell Miles the theory about the bandage, wanting him to convince her all was well, rather than giving him fresh reason for doubts.

"Too bad you're alone in this barn of a house, especially in the circumstances. It was very cavalier of Edward to fly off and leave you when you'd only just arrived."

"Oh, the trip to Peru was planned long before our visit. It was just—" She broke off, twisting her wedding ring round her finger. "My marriage has just ended, and Edward thought I'd like a change of scene."

Miles raised an eyebrow. "I wouldn't have credited him with such concern. Or did they want you to housekeep in their absence?"

Discounting her own initial surprise, Jan said reprovingly, "It was a very kind thought." She hesitated. "I gather you and he don't see eye to eye?"

"You could say that."

"Any specific reason?" She recalled Rowena saying Miles had been "offensive."

He shrugged. "A clash of personalities, aggravated by Rowena's resentment of my closeness to Mary."

Jan could accept that; there hadn't seemed much bond between Rowena and her mother over Christmas. "But she was always closer to her father, wasn't she?" she said. "Going with him on his expeditions, and everything."

"Oh yes," said Miles with controlled savagery, "those god-damned expeditions."

Jan threw him a startled glance, but he straightened, forestalling any comment. "You say your marriage has ended. You're divorced?"

"Not yet."

"I'm sorry, I didn't mean to pry."

"I know."

The clock on the mantelpiece whirred preparatory to striking. Jan saw it was eleven o'clock. Miles followed her glance.

"I'd better be going."

"It's so kind of you to have come. I did need to talk."

"Feel any better for it?"

She smiled. "A bit."

"Good." He got to his feet. "Let me know if you hear any more about this mysterious corpse. Not that I suppose you will. After such a wildly improbable start, no doubt the whole thing will fizzle out into something run-of-the-mill like gang warfare."

"That's run-of-the-mill?" Jan asked, with raised eyebrows.

He smiled. "You've been away a long time."

"I'm beginning to realize how long."

"Don't let it get you down. I'm at the end of the phone if you need me."

She watched him walk down the drive. Then she closed the door, double-locking and bolting it as Edward had instructed. For the first time, she was grateful that he and Rowena had gone to such lengths to safeguard their home.

The early morning was bitingly cold. The sky, only just lightening, was still streaked with red, the colour luridly reflected in the thin layer of ice which coated a pothole. The uniformed men detailed to preserve the scene stamped their feet and blew inside their gloves and the police dogs in the back of the van clouded the glass with their warm breath.

Webb stood watching the Scenes of Crime team, already re-engaged on work which darkness had interrupted the previous night.

"From the position of the body, I'd say he was simply tipped out of a car," commented Inspector Hodges. "Not much attempt at concealment. If it hadn't been for the tree, he'd have been spotted straight away."

"Which the murderer might have intended for some reason, or simply not given a damn about." Webb turned to look at the road. They were two miles short of the village of Chedbury, whose woods had yielded another murder victim some years previously. This part of the road lay between open fields, and the back of the layby could only be seen from directly opposite. Late at night, there wouldn't be much passing traffic. Now, however, a few early commuters were already driving in the direction of Shillingham, slowing down as they passed to stare curiously at the police activity.

"When did the gales start, anyone remember?"

"Night of the eighteenth," volunteered Jackson. "I know, because the twins were teething and Millie had to get up to them. The wind was howling round the house, and I thought, 'This time next week, Christmas'll be all over.' "

"And it was the eighteenth that this London journalist was due. Looks as though he could be our man."

"But it couldn't have been him that took the wallets, back in November."

"Unless he came over regularly. I hope to God this girl knows who he was coming to see." Webb turned to the dog-handlers. "OK, give them the scent and let them go. What we're looking for is anything which might be buried nearby—clothes, even—please God—a diary or notebook."

"Right, guv." The van door was opened and the two dogs jumped down. As they moved away, the animals straining eagerly at the leash, a uniformed constable approached.

"Excuse me, guv, there's still some coffee in the Thermos, if you'd like some."

"That would be very welcome, thank you. PC Linton, isn't it?"

"That's right, sir. We were on a case together a few years back."

"Yes, I was just thinking of it. Comes of Chedbury being the nearest bit of open countryside hereabouts." They moved over to one of the Panda cars and stood with their hands cupped round polystyrene cups, sipping the scalding liquid.

Suddenly, over the frosty fields, came the sound of a dog's excited barking. They all looked at each other expectantly.

"That was quick!" Linton exclaimed.

"If he'd been in a hurry, he wouldn't have had time to dig deep. Get the spades and let's see what they've found."

Twenty minutes later, a pile of clothes, clogged with earth and mould, lay on a plastic sheet on the frozen ground. At first sight, there appeared to be no identifying papers among them. Webb glanced at his watch. "We must get back—these people from London are due. Let me know what the lab makes of this lot, Dick. I'll be waiting with bated breath."

Webb's heart sank as soon as he saw the girl. Not the type to make a reliable witness, he thought gloomily. Still, she must know *something*, and at least she'd positively identified the body. The WDS from London led her over to a chair and stood protectively beside her, a hand on her shoulder. Webb said irritably, "All right, Sergeant, you can take a seat. We'll go easy with her. Now, Miss Potts, have a sip of tea and then we'd like you to answer some questions."

The girl gulped, sniffed, and nodded.

"How well did you know Mr. Marriott?"

Her eyes brimmed again. "We were living together, weren't we?"

"For how long?"

She shrugged. "Three months—maybe four."

"And he was a journalist?"

"Yeh—freelance. That means not for any particular paper," she added helpfully.

"Quite. If you could tell us some of the ones who published him?"

She mentioned three or four, and Jackson noted them down.

"And did he use a notebook, or pocket recorder?"

"Both. He always had both on him." There'd been neither with the body. "Sometimes he'd tease me by leaving the recorder switched on at the flat, and then playing it back." She bit her lip and looked away.

"Tell me about the last time you saw him."

"Well, it was before Christmas, and we were going to buy my present the next day during my lunch-hour. But then Guy says he can't meet me after all, because he's got to go to Broadshire." She gave a hiccuping little sob at the memory.

"He didn't say where in Broadshire?"

She looked vague. "I don't think so."

Webb sighed, and tried another tack. "Presumably he'd have come by car?"

"Oh yes."

"Well, if you could give us the make and number—" He broke off at her blank look.

"It was a blue one, two-door," she said. "I don't know the number."

"Or the make?"

She shook her head.

"That's not much help, then." Webb felt rather than saw the woman sergeant stiffen defensively. Obviously considered him a clumsy bumpkin, he thought resentfully.

He tried again. "If he broke a date to come over, surely he explained why?"

She looked stricken. "He did start to tell me, but I was watching telly and told him to shut up."

Webb held in his frustration. "Tell me what you do remember."

"It was about the story he was working on."

"And what story was that?"

Shirley Potts gazed at him desperately. Her anxiety to help was palpable, as was her inability to do so. "I don't know," she whispered.

Webb kept his voice steady. "Can you think of *any* stories he'd been working on recently? Please, Miss Potts, this could be very important."

She frowned and the tip of her tongue appeared, like a child trying to concentrate. "There was one about a film star who'd come to London."

"When was that?"

"Oh, during the summer, I suppose. I think he'd finished that one. And there was something about the Government, but I wasn't interested, so he didn't bother telling me."

"Was he still working on it?"

"I don't think so. And there was *something*—" She strained desperately after an elusive memory. "About famous people, he said."

"What kind of famous people?"

"Who'd done something wrong."

Investigative journalism, Webb thought heavily. That, he could do without. No knowing what you might stir up, and no thanks for it, either, as likely as not.

"A series of articles, about different people?"

"I think so."

"How many had he done?"

"I don't know." Sensing his frustration, she burst out, "Oh, I'm sorry! I do want to help, honest! Of *course* I want you to get whoever did this to Guy, but I just didn't *listen*, see! How did I know he was going to get himself killed?" And she broke into noisy sobs. With a black look in his direction, the woman sergeant rose and went to her, murmuring comfort.

Webb, wiping his hand over his face, conceded defeat. "All right, Miss Potts. Now, is there anywhere you can stay for the next few days? Scenes of Crime officers will want to examine your flat—they'll be waiting there when you get back."

She looked bewildered. "I suppose I could stay with Amy. You mean I have to move out?"

"Just for a few days. If you'll give us the address and phone number where you can be contacted, there's no need to keep you any longer. Thank you for your help."

Jan hadn't said anything to Lily about the previous evening. She didn't know the woman well, and there was no point in alarming her. If the connection with Edward was mentioned in the press, that would be time enough. But remembering last night's fears, she resolved to familiarize herself with the position of light switches, and since the children had complained the house was "spooky," they could accompany her and set their own fears at rest.

Accordingly they set off after breakfast on a tour of inspection, and by the end of it, Jan was forced to concede that there were indeed a lot of dark passages, and, though she made no comment on the fact, a disproportionate number of exits and entrances. Mentally she listed them: front and back door, French windows in drawing-room (which Edward had assured her were sealed), side door to the garden from the dining-room, cellar door accessible from the back garden, and even a coal chute, long disused. The bolts looked rusty, but Jan doubted they were covered by the burglar alarm. And Ben was right, there *were* spooky bits, down the back hall and around the cellar steps. The cellars themselves, lit by bare electric bulbs, were merely depressing, with their rows of empty Kilner jars gathering dust. Jan remembered her mother's pride in filling them each year with jams, pickles, and chutneys.

"It's not like the basement at home, is it, Mummy?" Julie said, with a wobble in her voice, and Jan could only agree it was not.

Something brushed against her and she jumped, looking down to see the cat's sinuous body winding itself round her legs. In the absence of her owners, Lotus was acting as hostess on their tour. She was a beautiful animal and seemed to have accepted their presence, but Jan would have been happier with a guard dog.

With an effort, she pulled herself together. There was no point in being neurotic about this. She had doubted the need for Edward's precautions when he'd explained them—why should the body of an unknown man have changed anything?

Leaving the children to explore the attics alone, Jan stopped off at the kitchen, where Lily was about to make some coffee.

The cat, purring loudly, transferred its attentions to her. Lily laughed. "Ready for your top-of-the-milk, are you? I'll bring your coffee to the library, Mrs. Coverdale."

"I'll have it here, Lily, if you don't mind."

"Oh, of course not." The woman's evident surprise, and the haste with which she cleared a space on the table, led Jan to suspect that Rowena didn't engage in such democratic practices.

"Have you been working here long?" she asked conversationally, accepting the cup of coffee.

"Several years now. I never knew your parents, though."

"And you always come in every day when my brother and his wife are away?"

"Oh yes. Mr. Langley's very particular about that. Says it makes the house look occupied. That's why he was so glad you decided to come."

Perhaps Miles had been right, Jan reflected a little sadly. At the very least, it seemed the arrangement was of mutual benefit.

"You usually have to go to your breeder's, don't you, my lady?" Lily was continuing, setting down a saucer of milk which the cat began to lap at daintily. "It suits you very nicely, too, having the family here."

"So you have to manoeuvre the burglar alarm every day?"

The woman smiled. "That's right. Scared me silly at first, but I'm used to it now."

"How long has it been in?" Jan asked casually, wondering why it mattered.

"We've only had this one about three years. Mr. Langley says it's more sophisticated than the last one."

"I can understand his taking precautions, but surely there's nothing exceptionally valuable in the house?"

"As to that, I couldn't say, ma'am. Lots of nice things, there are, but as to value, I've no idea. And of course there's a lot more crime about than you probably remember."

"So I've discovered," Jan acknowledged with a shudder, and ignored the woman's interrogatively raised eyebrows.

She finished her coffee and went through to the library.

Knowing Edward was actually in Peru had reawakened her interest, and she was skimming her way through the collection of books on it, some of which, having belonged to her father, she remembered from her own childhood.

Lost in the intricacies of the Quitan Campaign, she had no idea how much later it was that Julie's voice, high-pitched and excited, sounded from upstairs.

"Mummy! *Mummy!*"

Jan ran out into the hall as Lily appeared at the entrance to the passage.

"What is it? What's the matter?"

Both children were standing at the top of the stairs, Ben's hand gripping his sister's arm. Their faces were flushed and their eyes wide and bright. Jan stared up at them.

"What's the matter?" she repeated.

It seemed to her that Ben's hand tightened its grip. After a moment Julie said awkwardly, "Nothing. I just wondered where you were."

"Well, there was no need to shout like that. Lily and I thought you'd hurt yourself." She paused, something in the children's manner disturbing her. "Are you sure you're all right? Where have you been?"

Again the uncertain pause, then Ben said defensively, "Only playing."

"But where?"

"We've been up in the attics."

For a moment longer the four of them stood motionless, watching each other. Then, with an exasperated sigh, Jan turned away. "Well, for heaven's sake behave yourselves," she said.

CHAPTER 5

Webb said, "I'm curious about those wallets. Who, in their right mind, nicks four, returns three, and leaves the fourth in the pocket of a corpse? Give Court Lane a buzz, Ken, and get the names and addresses of the other three owners. We'll go down and have a word with them." He turned to Stanley Bates. "Anything of interest during my lunch break?"

"We drew a blank on the car-parks." Bates permitted himself a tight smile. "There were a fair number of blue, two-door cars, but they'd all clocked in this morning."

"We'll have to spread our net wider, then. It's always possible the murderer drove off in Marriott's car, in which case it could be anywhere."

"Such as hidden in a private garage," Jackson said gloomily. "We might never find it." And he went out to make his phone call.

Bates gave a small cough. "If you like, skip, I could nip down to Broadminster, seeing as I went yesterday, and save you the trip."

"Thanks, Stan, but I need to see these blokes myself. I'm relying on you to keep things going this end," he added diplomatically. "We want photos of Marriott circulated, for a start, to see if we can trace anyone who saw him on the eighteenth. Get one round to Romilly at *The Broadshire News*. Then I'd be grateful if you'd phone the London papers Miss Potts mentioned. Say I'll be up tomorrow, and will want to see all the articles Marriott wrote in the last six months, particularly the famous people series. I'll also be wanting the names of any reporters or journalists he was friendly with, and a note of where I can find them."

He frowned, tapping his pen on the desk. "How many 'famous people' would you say we have in Broadshire, Stan?"

"Depends what you mean by famous. We've our fair share of writers, artists, and, of course, members of Parliament. Not forgetting the explorers down in Broadminster, though Edward Langley and his wife are the only ones left now."

Webb said slowly, "It seems Marriott came over to interview a celebrity who was up to something dubious. He was found dead with Langley's wallet in his pocket. Langley is a celebrity. Do we assume it was Langley he came to see?"

Bates pursed his lips. "Langley wouldn't put his own head in a noose. And don't forget he didn't *have* the wallet at that point."

"Unless he'd nicked it himself, to throw suspicion elsewhere. It's significant it was the only one not to turn up almost immediately."

Bates felt in his pocket, extracted a foil sheet of indigestion tablets, and pressed two of them into the palm of his hand. It occurred to Webb he'd seen the same ritual before.

"You hooked on those things, Stan?"

"Been having a spot of trouble lately, skip. Touch of dyspepsia, I suppose."

At least it wasn't the drink, Webb reflected morosely, returning to the papers on his desk. For the second time, he read the preliminary report on the items found with the body. The bandage was a standard type, available at chemists throughout the country; coarse black thread had been used to sew on the sequins, and the clumsiness of the stitches suggested a man's hand; scraps of newspaper had been found adhering to the inside of the sweater, trousers, and jacket, which, under examination, proved to have come from *The Times* for Monday the third of November. Webb raised an eyebrow at that point.

"Are the quality newspapers warmer next to the skin than the populars?" he asked rhetorically, and was irritated when Bates gave the question consideration.

"Quite possibly, skip. Pricier, though."

"Not if retrieved from a litter bin."

A tap on the door heralded Jackson, his eyes alight. "Bit of luck, guv," he said eagerly. "Court Lane were on the point of phoning us. They've got the car."

"In Broadminster?"

"That's right. It was in the High Street multi-storey—clocked in at fourteen-ten on December 18. When it was still there the next morning, they got on to Court Lane, who phoned Swansea and found Marriott was the owner, but they were unable to contact him. Then the Missing Persons alert came through, and they've been looking for him ever since."

"Why the hell didn't they mention it yesterday?"

"Because we told them we'd got Edward Langley. They didn't see the connection."

Webb swore softly. "How the devil did he get from Broadminster to Chedbury without the car? Courtesy of his killer, no doubt, but it's a hell of a way to take him. Were there any car-keys with the things we found this morning?"

Jackson flicked open his notebook. "No, guv."

"They were probably dropped down a drain somewhere. The killer couldn't have known where it was parked. Right, Ken; if Broadminster was where Marriott made for, it's increasingly likely he came to see Langley. In which case, another talk with his sister won't go amiss."

"Of course," Bates cut in, "it could have been the other way round."

"Explain."

"Well, skip, you said yourself the killer could have moved the car. Marriott might have come to Shillingham, got the chop, and been dumped at Chedbury—which, don't forget, is much nearer here. Then the murderer could have driven Marriott's car to Broadminster, to divert suspicion."

"You're right, of course," Webb said heavily. "But since we have to make a start somewhere, we'll begin in Broadminster. Did you get the names and addresses of the wallet-owners, Ken?"

"Yes, they're all here."

"We'll be on our way, then."

Jan said, "Oh, Lady Peel! You're back."

"Miles met me at the station. My dear, I hear you've had a most worrying time. I'm so sorry I wasn't here to help."

"It could have been worse. At least it wasn't Edward."

"Would you like to bring the children to tea? I was intending to invite you in a day or two, but in the circumstances I'd rather see you now, and set my mind at rest."

"We'd love to come. Thank you."

"In about an hour, then?"

Jan returned to the library, and glanced at the children lying on the rug. They had stayed with her since lunch, instead of going off to play as they usually did. Several times she'd intercepted mouthed messages passing between them when they thought she wasn't looking. She said brightly, "We're going to Cajabamba for tea."

A uniformed maid opened the door to them, and Lady Peel appeared in the hall behind her. "Come in, my dears, and get warm. I suggest we have tea first, then we can have our little talk."

There were fingers of hot-buttered toast, newly baked scones, and a jam sponge. Almost the same fare, Jan could have sworn, as on her childhood visits here. The children, whose normal appetite had been lacking at lunch-time, devoured all that was set before them. When they had finished, Lady Peel led them over to a table she had set up at the far end of the room. On it was a collection of toys and puzzles dating from Rowena's youth, together with miniature dolls and animals. The children drew up chairs and settled down happily and Lady Peel returned to Jan by the fire.

"I think they're beyond earshot, if we speak quietly," she said with a smile. "Now, my dear, please tell me exactly what happened."

Once again, Jan went over the happenings of the previous evening. "It was very kind of Miles to come round," she ended. "I was feeling shaken and—vulnerable, and it helped to talk things through."

"It's a most curious story," Lady Peel said with a frown, "Edward's wallet turning up in such unlikely circumstances. However did that tramp get hold of it?"

"I'm not sure that he was a tramp," Jan said slowly.

"You say he had a look of Edward. That strikes me as a trifle sinister."

"That's what I thought, but Miles seemed to think it was coincidence." She paused, then added irrelevantly, "He's very fond of you, isn't he?"

Lady Peel smiled. "It's mutual. He's like the son I never had."

"Didn't you help to bring him up, or something?"

"That's right. Poor Isabelle was neurotic and quite unable to cope with a child. We lived in Surrey at that time, and the Coadys in London, but our families were thrown together a great deal, what with the expeditions being planned, and so on. And more and more often, Isabelle would ask me to look after Miles for her. We had a nanny, so it was no trouble." She smiled fondly. "Except that he used to follow me everywhere I went. Rowena was a self-contained child, quite happy to stay in the nursery with Nanny, but Miles seemed to need my company. I don't mind admitting I was flattered."

"And then what happened?" Jan prompted.

"Well, then there was the ill-fated third expedition. Your father was brought home seriously ill, and both Reginald and Laurence were under considerable strain. It was felt it would be easier to liaise in the future if we all lived closer together. Your family was already settled here, so we and the Coadys moved down too. I think Laurence felt it might be less stressful for Isabelle away from London, but alas, it didn't help her, poor girl. She took her own life soon afterwards."

"I didn't know that!" Jan exclaimed.

"No, of course you didn't, and I probably shouldn't be telling you now. We never spoke of it. And after her death, poor Laurence withdrew more and more into himself. It was at that stage that I volunteered to take over Miles's welfare. He was about eight by then, and already showing artistic talent. He's doing exceptionally well, you know, and making quite a name for himself. He appeared on a television arts programme last month."

But Jan was more interested in his father. "Was that why Laurence never went back to Peru?"

"Quite possibly."

"But it doesn't explain why my father didn't, either. I've been wondering about that."

Lady Peel said slowly, "He'd been very ill, you know."

"But he recovered. And Sir Reginald kept going back. Didn't he try to persuade the others to join him?"

"I really don't remember, my dear. It does seem odd, looking back, that your father and Laurence dropped out, but at the time we accepted it as quite natural."

"So after all the trouble of moving to make it easier, there *were* no more joint expeditions."

"True, but they still saw a great deal of each other. My husband and Laurence were always calling at Rylands."

"At least I understand now why you were all down here. It seemed strange, three famous explorers just happening to live in Broadminster, which isn't exactly the hub of the universe. In fact, I started to ask Edward about it, my first night here, but I was too sleepy to think straight." Her thoughts came back to the present, which was no less puzzling, and she spoke them aloud. "He had a very tight bandage round his arm—put on after death, the police say. Can you think of any reason for it?"

For a moment Lady Peel looked startled. Then she said, "Oh, you mean this tramp person. How most peculiar."

"But does it bring anything to mind?" Jan persisted.

"I don't understand, dear. What could it bring to mind, other than that it was an illogical action by a psychopath?"

Jan sighed. "You're probably right," she said.

"Number 7, Clarence Mews," Jackson said, checking in his notebook. "It must be down here, then."

They had turned off the High Street into Clarence Way, which led up to Monks' Walk and the Minster. Three-quarters of the way along, a cobbled courtyard led off to the right, and it was here, according to Court Lane, that the third wallet-owner, Miles Coady, lived.

"Probably won't have any more luck here," Jackson grumbled. It had not been a successful afternoon. There'd been no one in at the Langley house, and the two wallet-owners they'd tried so far were not at home, either. "My husband doesn't get in till six," they'd been told reproachfully at each house. He peered at his watch under the light of an old-fashioned street lamp which lit the entrance to the mews. "Quarter after five." He wouldn't be back for the twins' bath tonight.

But when they'd threaded their way over the uneven cobbles and turned the corner into the yard, the diamond-paned windows of number 7 glowed with a soft light.

"Somebody's in, anyway," Jackson commented, his spirits rising. With any luck, they might be offered a cup of tea. It seemed a long time since lunch.

The man who came to the door was as tall as Webb, his features indistinguishable against the light behind him.

"Yes?"

"Mr. Miles Coady?"

"That's right."

"Chief Inspector Webb, Shillingham CID. I wonder if we could have a word, sir?"

"Good God! What about?"

"About your wallet that was stolen a month or two ago."

"But I got it back. Didn't they tell you? There's no—"

"If we could come inside for a minute, sir? We won't take up much of your time."

"Very well." He stood to one side, and the two detectives went in. The door opened directly into the only main room the cottage possessed. But what a room! Jackson thought; a positive Aladdin's cave of warmth and colour. A log fire crackled merrily in an open brick hearth, and at the far end, steps led up to a railed balcony which, as far as he could see, served as the bedroom.

"Can I get you a drink?" asked Miles Coady. In the light of the huge, ornate light-fitting which hung from the ceiling, he looked to be in his late thirties, with dark, slightly long hair, thick black eyebrows, and a dark shave. He was wearing a silk cravat in the neck of a coffee-coloured shirt, and brown cord trousers. An artist, Jackson told himself. No two ways about it.

"Some tea would be very welcome, sir."

Coady's eyebrow went up, but he made no comment. He opened what looked like a cupboard door, to reveal a pocket-sized kitchen, complete with cooker, sink, and fridge.

"How could my returned wallet be of any interest to Shillingham?" he asked, as he filled a kettle.

"We'd like to hear in exactly what circumstances you came to lose it, sir, and exactly how it was recovered."

"Well, that's easy enough. It was taken from the squash club changing-room, and pushed through the letter-box of the club a couple of days later. Together, as far as I remember, with others that were stolen at the same time."

"But not all of them," Webb said significantly.

"Ah—light is dawning. I hear you've found Edward Langley's."

Webb's eyes narrowed. "How do you know about that, sir?" The full story would be in tomorrow's papers, but no details had appeared as yet.

"It's quite simple. I had a call from Janis Coverdale."

Webb relaxed. "I see, sir. A friend, is she?"

"Of sorts. Our fathers were fellow-explorers in the dim and distant past."

"Is that so? I hadn't realized. You were never bitten by the bug yourself, sir?"

"Most definitely not. As far as I'm concerned, the very word 'Peru' is a turn-off."

"You know, of course, that Mr. Langley's there at the moment?"

"Of course."

"And Mrs. Coverdale rang to tell you about his wallet."

"She rang, Chief Inspector, to ask me to accompany her to identify what she was given to understand was her brother's body. I wasn't in, but she left a message on the answer-phone."

It fitted. Bates had said the woman made a phone call. Coady poured boiling water into a stone teapot and brought it, a couple of mugs, and a milk jug over to a low table. It seemed he wouldn't be joining them.

"Who was at the club when the wallets were taken?"

"The usual Saturday crowd. The courts had been booked all morning, and we were the last four to play. But the bar was full, and anyone could have slipped through without being noticed. There was an overlap of about ten minutes when we were all on court. Then Cassidy and I finished, showered, and went through to the bar."

"Without having missed your wallets?"

"Yes. I only realized when I reached in my pocket to pay for some drinks."

"So you were the first to discover the loss?"

"It was more or less simultaneous. Cassidy immediately felt for his, and we were just registering what must have happened when the others burst in from the changing-room with the news that theirs had gone, too." He paused. "With respect, Chief Inspector, you can get all these details from your colleagues here."

"We have consulted with them, naturally," said Webb blandly, "but a first-hand account is always useful." He looked up and met the faintly mocking eyes. "You do realize, sir, in the light of the latest developments, that the thief could also be a murderer?"

There was a brief pause, then Coady said softly, "Touché. I see what you mean."

"Have you ever heard of a man called Guy Marriott, sir?"

"Is that the chap that was killed? No, I can't say I have."

"He was a journalist from London. We have reason to believe he came to Broadminster to interview someone."

"Broadminster? I thought he was found near Shillingham?"

"As a matter of routine, sir, where were you on Thursday the eighteenth of December?"

"I?" Coady stared at him. "What has this to do with me?"

"Just routine, sir. We'll be asking everyone we interview about the wallets. They had a link with the deceased, after all."

"A very tenuous one. In any case, I can't possibly remember after all this time. And why the eighteenth of December?"

"That was the date he came over."

"Oh yes—Janis said it was before Christmas."

"If you could try to remember, sir," Webb prompted gently.

"I work from home, Chief Inspector, and one day is much like another. Just before Christmas, I was extremely busy and made several visits to London, but I can't recall the dates."

"Wouldn't your diary help?"

Coady smiled. "Unfortunately, I threw it out on the first of January."

Webb sighed. "To come back to the wallets, then. There was no note, or any word of explanation when they were returned?"

"Not a thing."

"And the contents were intact?"

"As far as any of us could recall, absolutely."

Webb sipped his tea and looked round the ornate room. There were low tables with large lamps on them, and magazines piled haphazardly on the lower shelves. There was a marble bust on a plinth at the foot of the stairs to the balcony, and a very interesting oil painting above the fireplace. Quite a number of antiques, he'd say, but in the general clutter it was hard to be sure. At the end of the room, under the balcony, was a curtained window and beneath it a large desk and a series of bookcases.

"You say you work at home, sir?"

"Most of the time. I'm an illustrator, for what are known as coffee-table books. Theatrical décor mostly."

Webb's interest quickened. "So you're an artist?" A common interest might establish contact with what he felt to be an elusive character.

"I paint, yes, but I spend a fair proportion of my time taking photographs."

Reluctantly Webb abandoned an interesting discussion and returned to more relevant matters. "To come back to the squash club, was there anyone you didn't know there that day, anyone who hadn't been before?"

"Not that I recall. Again, I'd refer you to your colleagues. They went into that very exhaustively."

"Then I don't think we need keep you any longer, Mr. Coady." Webb rose to his feet. "Oh, one last point, since your father was an explorer. Would a tightly wrapped bandage put on after death have any significance to you?"

"Put on where? What part of the body?"

"Round an arm."

Coady shrugged. "If it had been all over, it would have suggested a mummy, but other than that, I couldn't say. Is that any help?"

"It might well be, Mr. Coady," Webb said slowly, "it might well be."

"Miles! What a lovely surprise!"

Jan turned, to see him standing in the doorway in his overcoat, his shoulders glistening with drops of moisture.

"I didn't know you had company."

"Come in, darling, and take your coat off. Janis and I are just having a chat, and the children, as you see, have been amusing themselves. Is it too early to offer you a drink?"

"Oh, I think not," he said with a smile. "Can I get one for anyone else?"

"Janis?" invited Lady Peel.

"I think it's time we were going home," Jan said. Miles hadn't expected to find them here; no doubt he wanted Lady Peel to himself.

But it was he who replied. "Nonsense; it's early yet. I'll walk you back later."

"That isn't necessary, I—"

"Don't argue, woman, and state your poison."

She subsided, smiling, and requested a gin and tonic.

"I thought you were working to a deadline," Lady Peel remarked. "Have you finished what you'd set yourself?"

Miles turned and carried the glasses across. "Not quite, but there was an interruption and it broke the thread. A visit from the police, no less."

"The police?"

"Janis's friends, from Shillingham. They wanted to hear about my stolen wallet."

"Oh, of course—they must be linking it with Edward's. How unpleasant for you."

"It didn't worry me, Mary. If they enjoy sitting in their big boots drinking tea, who am I to deny them? But I'm afraid I wasn't much help."

"It was a strange business, about those wallets," Lady Peel said reflectively. "I thought so at the time. There was no point in it. If they were taken for a joke, you'd expect the joker to declare himself. And if it was genuine, why was nothing taken from them?"

Jan stirred, suddenly chilled. "Perhaps," she said, "it was only Edward's he wanted, and the others were taken as a blind."

Lady Peel looked worried. Miles thought for a moment, then said, "But why take them at the beginning of November, when Edward's didn't show up till January?"

Jan shook her head. "It was only a thought. I hope I'm wrong."

"Have the police any theories?" Lady Peel asked Miles.

"If they have, they didn't favour me with them. The only information they volunteered was that there'd been a bandage on the body, which I already knew from Janis. Not that I told them so."

"That's curious, isn't it? We were just discussing it."

"They asked if it suggested anything to me." His eyes held Jan's.

"And what did you tell them?" she asked.

"Well, I'd had time to think about it since last night, so I said that had it been all over, it might have symbolized a mummy." Lady Peel's hand went to her throat, but Miles kept his eyes on Jan. "Did that also occur to you, by any chance?"

So despite not having voiced her fears the previous evening, Miles had arrived at the same conclusion.

"Yes," she said quietly, "it did."

"I was waiting for them to tell me about the sequins, but they didn't mention them."

"What sequins?" Lady Peel looked from one to the other. "What are you talking about?"

Jan said, "I'm sorry, Lady Peel, I didn't go into details. The fact was that the jacket the—the body was wearing had sequins sewn on it. And I'm wondering whether, if the bandage was supposed to make the police think of mummies, the sequins also had a meaning."

Lady Peel made a dismissive gesture with her hand. "I don't care for this at all," she said emphatically. "A murder's bad enough, goodness knows, but I object most strongly when the murderer plays games with the police. Bandages and sequins, indeed. It's—grotesque."

The children, hearing raised voices and in any case tiring of their games, came across to the fire, their eyes going from one intent adult face to the other.

God, Jan thought guiltily, I hope they didn't hear anything. She put an arm round each of them, drawing them to her sides. "It really is time we were going," she said firmly. "Thank Lady Peel for your tea, and for taking the trouble to find you things to play with."

"I'll walk home with you," Miles said again. He bent and kissed the older woman. "Don't worry about it, Mary. It'll sort itself out. I'll be in touch again soon."

It was dank and cold outside, with no moon. Despite herself, Jan was glad of Miles's company, though it was only an eight-minute walk. At the gate of Rylands, she said, "That was kind of you. Thank you."

He hesitated. "How would it be if I came in for a while, rather than both of us sitting alone? Or am I intruding?"

"No, of course not. I'd be glad of the company."

"Tell you what, then. I'll go and buy a bottle of wine while you put the children to bed, and we can continue our discussion over it."

So Jan and Miles spent a second evening together, but the

bandaged, besequined body wasn't mentioned again. Instead, as they ate supper by the library fire, Jan asked about his work, listening, fascinated, to his account of books he'd worked on and authors he'd met. He'd done the illustrations for a series of books on Stately Homes, and told some amusing anecdotes about their occupants; and he'd been abroad on several photographic assignments.

"As a matter of fact," he added, "this year looks like being particularly rewarding. I've been put in overall charge of all the artwork involved in the tercentennial celebrations of Buckhurst Grange."

"That sounds fantastic. What does it involve?"

"Just about everything. Designing posters, coordinating press releases, television advertisements, arranging exhibitions —even designing a set of commemorative stamps for the Post Office. It's by far the most exciting project I've ever worked on, and a tremendous responsibility. But if I handle it well—and I think I can—then my future's pretty well assured."

"That's wonderful, Miles," Jan said warmly. "What a fascinating life! No wonder you've not had time to get married!"

He laughed. "There's still time, if the mood takes me. I'd be a demanding husband, though. Perhaps no one would have me."

"You've never been tempted?"

"Once or twice, but I've managed to withstand it!" He glanced at her. "Would you recommend marriage?"

She sobered abruptly. "I'm not the best person to ask at the moment."

"Do you want to talk about it?"

"Not really. I'm still in a state of shock. You see, it never entered my head anything would go wrong. We were always so happy together."

"And what did go wrong?"

She grimaced. "The old, old story. A younger woman."

"My God, girl, you're not in your dotage!"

She smiled unwillingly. "Nevertheless, she's ten years younger than I am."

"But that couldn't have been the attraction, surely?"

"It was probably part of it. She hadn't two children to look after, and she was bubbly and full of life. She might even have reminded him of me when we first met. But I hadn't an inkling anything was wrong—possibly because for a long time Roger fought it, tried to stop it happening."

"And eventually he just upped and left?"

"Pretty well." She paused. "He phoned on Christmas Day. It was—weird to hear him again, and it upset the children, too."

"Are you still in love with him?"

"I suppose so, underneath. But on top is a lot of hurt and anger and resentment, which makes things very complicated."

"Poor Janis."

She said, "Could you call me 'Jan'? That's what I'm used to."

"Of course." He looked at his watch. "Time I was on my way."

"I suppose so. I've a full day ahead tomorrow; I'm taking the children to London, sight-seeing."

"Rather you than me." He stood up and stretched, his face going into the shadows above the fire. "Well, good night, Jan-not-Janis. Enjoy your trip to London. And thank you for supper."

"A pleasure," she said.

CHAPTER 6

Webb opened his eyes to see her setting the tray down on the table.

"Hannah, I'm sorry! It's been a hell of a day."

"No need to apologize—sorry I woke you. Are you ready to eat, or would you rather snooze a bit longer?"

"But you must be ravenous. What time is it?"

"Nearly ten. It has dried up a bit, but nothing drastic. I've learnt to stick to casseroles when you're working on a case."

He reached out a hand and she took it, smiling. Oh, thank God! he thought. Thank *God* they were back together again. There'd been a time, last summer, when he was sure he'd lost her, but it had come right in the end. And one thing was certain —he'd never again take her for granted. The shadow of Charles Frobisher, who'd had the nerve to ask her to marry him, was still an ever-present threat.

"Come on, then, sleeping beauty," she said, withdrawing her hand. "You'll feel better when you've eaten."

"And this was meant to be a celebration," he said ruefully, "after not seeing each other for two weeks."

"It still can be, if your eyes stay open! Is it the murdered tramp case? There hasn't been much in the papers."

"There will be tomorrow. And he wasn't a tramp, he was a London journalist. Trouble is, the action's split between here and Broadminster. Body found here—well, the Chedbury layby —but seeming to masquerade as a Broadminster man. Which, as I said, he wasn't."

Hannah laughed. "Not the clearest summary I've heard."

"Believe me, that's not the half of it."

"Tell me about your bad day."

He grimaced. "It started with the scene of crime at dawn, and proceeded, via a difficult session with the girl who identified him, to Broadminster. We wanted to interview one woman and three men—not, you'd have thought, a daunting prospect. But no one was where we expected them to be. We never caught up with the woman, and had to hang around till two of the men got back from work. All of which explains the ungodly hour I arrived here. I should have phoned and told you not to wait." He watched her spooning out the richly smelling casserole. "Have you ever heard of Edward Langley?"

"Of course I have. The Fourth Form did a project on his last expedition, following it on huge wall maps."

Webb said flatly, "I seem to be the only one in the entire county never to have heard of him."

"He's well-known on the lecture circuit, and did a series on TV a year or two back. He counts on the fees to help finance his expeditions. And I read his father's book, too, *The Hidden City*. Quite fascinating, all about the discovery in the fifties of an Inca city, completely buried under jungle growth."

Webb said curiously, "Was there a man called Coady on that expedition?"

"Of course—Coady, Langley, and Peel. Known, so I'm told, as the Three Caballeros. Coady was the best-known of them originally. It was he who talked the other two into going to Peru, and persuaded the International Inca Society to sponsor them."

"What a fund of information you are!" Webb said in mock admiration as he started on his casserole. "There are definite perks to relationships with teachers! I presume the original three are all dead now?"

"Sir Reginald only died a few months ago. You must have seen his obituaries."

Vaguely, now that he thought about it, Webb recalled an item on television news, a man's face, and pictures of jungles and mountains. It had meant nothing at the time.

"Why the sudden interest?"

"Because Edward Langley is involved in the case—I'm not sure yet how deeply—and I met Coady's son this afternoon."

"Really? I didn't even know he had one. He hasn't figured in any expeditions that I've heard of."

"Not interested," said Webb with his mouth full. "The whole thing's a turn-off, he said. You can understand it. It must have been rammed down his throat all his life."

"I suppose so. Especially with Peel's daughter joining him as soon as she was old enough."

Webb looked up. "And *I* hadn't heard of *her*. Is she still around?"

"Very definitely. She's married to Edward Langley."

"Ye gods!"

"But how can Langley be involved in your case? He's in Peru at the moment."

"Ah, but the body was dumped before he left, and has only just come to light. He *could* have done it." He paused. "Anyway, let's change the subject. I've reached saturation point on this for the moment. How long have you left of your grossly extended Christmas holiday?"

Hannah laughed. "Sour grapes! We don't go back till the fifteenth, but I've a lot to do before then, planning timetables and checking on syllabuses. I'm not as idle as you seem to think."

"To paraphrase Citizen Kane, it might be amusing to own a school."

"I'm only Deputy Head, remember. Amusing's not the word I'd choose, but it's certainly interesting."

Webb topped up her wine glass and his own. He'd have liked to inquire whether she'd seen Charles Frobisher lately, if he was still Chairman of the Board of Governors, but he didn't dare. Still, he'd nothing to complain of. When it had come to the crunch, Frobisher had lost and he'd won. God knows why, but he was humbly grateful.

He looked up, met her considering eyes, and grinned. "It's a superb casserole. Next time, I won't worry if I'm two hours late!"

She'd been dreaming of Roger again, dreaming they were preparing the barbecue in the hot sunshine, while the children raced each other across the pool. How safe, how *happy*, she'd felt in her dream. No Pam Stevens, with her high, excited giggles, to lure him away. No dead Edward look-alikes dressed in sequins and bandages. Just Roger, the children, and herself, as it had always been, as it had seemed it always would be. She woke with tears on her face to an impatient rattling of the door handle.

"Mummy! It's time to get up!"

Hastily she dried her cheeks. "I shan't be long. Feed Lotus for me, will you, and lay the breakfast table. Lily should be here soon."

The day awaited her; not a lazy, sunfilled one, scented with charcoal and succulent steaks and sun-warmed bodies, but a cold, winter day during which she must trail into London with the children. With a sigh, she reluctantly swung her legs out of bed.

"Still popping pills, Stan? You should see the quack."

"I had a bad night, skip—felt decidedly queasy. Might go along to the surgery later, if it doesn't clear up." He handed a file to Webb.

"The editor of the *Courier* said you're in luck; he's expecting Lewis Daly to look in mid-day. Apparently he was quite thick with Marriott. And they all said they'd look up the articles you want."

"Fine," said Webb absently, skimming through the papers. "And Romilly'll run the photo tonight?"

"Yes, no problem there." Bates paused. "He told me to ask if you'd any more cartoons. Said he hadn't had anything for months." Bates eyed his superior curiously, knowing better than to venture a direct question.

Webb cursed softly. The cartoons were drawn for his own amusement, but every now and then Mike Romilly swooped and bore them off for publication in *The News*. Fair enough, and the money was useful, but the signature—the circled "S" by which

Webb wryly depicted a spider in a web—was supposed to guard their anonymity.

He was saved from replying by Jackson's arrival, and leaving Bates palely at his desk, they set off at once for London.

Jan said, "There's no need for you to stay, Lily. If you could just bank up the library fire, that'll be fine."

"Thank you, ma'am, but I've a few things to do before I go. Don't worry, I'll switch on the alarm when I leave. Enjoy yourselves in London."

"It'll be pretty exhausting, I imagine. Where are the children? I thought they were ready hours ago." She went to the foot of the stairs and called. Julie came running down alone.

"Ben's trying to get at Lotus. She's on the roof under his window."

With a sigh, Jan hurried upstairs and along to the old nursery. The window sash was pushed up and her son was leaning precariously outside.

"Ben! Come inside at once and close that window! The room's like a fridge!"

"But Lotus is out there—she can't get down!"

"Of course she can get down." Jan went to the window. The flat roof of the storeroom was some four feet below, and on it, the cat sat unconcernedly licking itself. Jan pushed the window down and fastened the catch.

"She'll get down when she wants to, don't worry. Now come along, or we'll miss the train."

She hurried out of the room. Ben hesitated, turned back, and unfastening the window, pushed it up six inches. Then he ran after his mother.

Webb looked disparagingly at the Bayswater building. "Every time I come to London, I'm more glad I live in Shillingham!" he said. "OK, Ken, let's go up and see how the SOCOs are getting on."

The Scenes of Crime officers were London-based, and Webb

didn't know them personally. He introduced himself to the senior man. "How's it going?"

"Slowly, as always. Not much personal stuff, and the girl said
he'd no other home. Moved in with her when the lease ran out
on his last place."

"So what have you got?"

"Only real source of information was the desk." He nodded
towards a cheap one against the far wall. "Note pads in shorthand—they're being transcribed, but first impressions indicate
they're out of date. He probably had his current one on him."

"Not when he was found, unfortunately, nor his pocket recorder."

"There are some cassettes, too, which we're working on.
Other than that, engagement diary, address book, cheque stubs,
and bank statements. They're being photo-copied and should
be with you tomorrow."

"Copy of a will?"

"Not so far."

"Can't have everything, I suppose. Mind if we look around?
We'll try not to get in your way."

"Help yourself."

It was a characterless room, with the necessities of living
haphazardly arranged: sofa, arm chair, gate-legged table, all of
them nondescript and needing attention. The television stood
in pride of place, apparently the most valued item in the room.
Above the gas fire hung a cheap print of a Mediterranean scene
—ochre-yellow houses, mules, a cobbled street. A pile of newspapers was stacked against a wall, and various women's magazines littered the coffee table. Of what Webb considered
"proper books," there was no sign. As the SOCO had indicated,
the only likely source of interest was the desk.

Trying not to disturb the men working, they moved from one
room to another. The double bed was unmade, the surface of
the dressing-table covered with half-empty jars, most of them
without lids. On the kitchen sink, a thick yellow crust encircled
the milk-bottle top, filling the room with its rancid odour. Yet

none of the possessions littering the flat gave any indication of the interests of its occupants.

It was with a feeling of relief that they left its depressing anonymity and made their way to Fleet Street.

"It was one hell of a shock," said Lewis Daly, finishing his pint. "I still can't believe it."

They were sitting in the Printers' Ink discussing the demise of Guy Marriott.

"When was the last time you saw him?" Webb inquired.

"Can't remember exactly. Not long before Christmas; we were lunching here, actually. He was full of a new lead he'd come across, but wouldn't say what it was. Typical, that. Old Guy was like a clam when he was on to a story. No use pumping him, you had to bide your time. But once it was in print under his byline, he'd regale you with all the trials and tribulations he went through to get it, often with highly actionable asides as to the integrity and antecedents of his sources."

"So it's no use asking anyone else what he was on to?"

Daly shook his head. "I was as close to him as anyone."

"Can you remember his exact words?"

Daly considered. "He was in high spirits. He lifted his glass and said, 'To the righting of wrongs!' I laughed, and said, 'Does that mean you're after another poor bastard?' And he grinned and said, 'No, a rich one! I've just had a break, Lew. He won't be able to wriggle out of this one.' And I said, 'You just watch it, my lad. One of these days you'll come across someone who'll bite back when you try to poke your nose in his affairs.' God, if I'd only known."

He paused, and repeated slowly, " 'To the righting of wrongs.' He meant that, you know. All right, so the money was good, but he believed in what he was doing."

Webb made no comment on the philosophy. Instead, he asked, "Did he say where this man lived?"

Daly shook his head.

"And that was the last time you saw him?"

"Yep. A crowd of us had arranged a get-together later that

week, but Guy didn't show up. I didn't think anything of it. Shirley was apt to be possessive and sulked if he went drinking with the lads."

"And this exposé series was the only one he was working on at the time?"

"As far as I know, yes."

Which was where they had to leave it. None of the editors they saw that afternoon could add anything to what Lewis Daly had told them. Marriott was known to play his hand close to his chest —understandable in a competitive field, but the editors were unanimous in agreeing he was a first-class journalist. There was a general air of gloom at his death, which said as much for the man as for his work. But someone had seen Guy Marriott in a very different light.

"It's a dangerous game, Ken," Webb commented as they drove home with Marriott's press-cuttings piled on the back seat. "All very well to fancy yourself a crusader, but not everyone sees it that way, least of all if he's on the receiving end."

He bent forward, peering through the windscreen as they came onto the Hammersmith Flyover. "Don't tell me it's starting to snow."

"Looks like it, guv. Lord knows it's been cold enough."

Webb sighed. "Roll on the spring. Right, so who have we got in this case? One dead journalist, one absent explorer, and three blokes whose wallets were pinched. Not a lot to go on."

"We've also got some unknown quantities," Jackson commented, switching on the windscreen wipers. "Such as X who stole the wallets and Y who killed Marriott. Or XY who did both."

Webb grunted. "What about the blokes we saw yesterday? They live in Broadminster, and they were on hand when the wallets were stolen."

"So was the rest of the squash club. That doesn't make them murderers."

"Damn it, Ken, what else have we got?"

"Well, Edward Langley comes into it somewhere. The killer

wanted us to think it was him, and he was still around on the eighteenth of December."

"And on that day, Cassidy and Rollo went to work as usual. But since they both work in Broadminster, that doesn't rule out meeting Marriott. As for Miles Coady, he may or may not have been home." His voice quickened. "Look, we've been assuming Marriott came to see this crooked celebrity. But suppose he was visiting someone else, the man who supplied the information?"

"Then why was he killed?"

"God knows." The excitement went out of Webb's voice. "We still need to see Mrs. Coverdale. If she can remember her brother's movements on the eighteenth, it could be useful. We'll give that first priority tomorrow. That is," he finished, staring out at the large white flakes that were now plastering the windscreen, "always provided we're not snowed up by tomorrow."

Jan too, on her homeward journey, was watching the snow through the train window. The further west they went, the thicker it seemed to fall, and it was already lying in an even coat over the Wiltshire fields. The children, never having seen snow before, found it more exciting than all the historical sights they'd seen. They were in a frenzy of anxiety that it might disappear before they had a chance to play out in it and make a snowman.

As Jan had anticipated, she was exhausted, but it had been an interesting day. London was busier than she remembered, a combination of the continuing school holidays and the January sales. It had meant repeated queuing, and as a result there hadn't been time for everything she'd planned.

Still, they'd covered quite a lot, and they could always go again. Her mind went back over the day: Westminster Abbey, St. Paul's; but the Tower had been the most successful visit. The children were entranced by the ravens and Traitors' Gate; Ben studied every suit of armour in the White Tower, and had insisted on having his photo taken with a yeoman on guard duty. Yet when, after a long wait in a queue, they came at last to the Crown Jewels, Julie's reaction, at least, had been surprising.

True, both children had gazed wide-eyed at the various crowns, at the orb and sceptre and swords. But when Jan paused in front of a case of exquisite bracelets and necklaces, Julie had turned away. "They're not as nice as Aunt Rowena's," she said dismissively.

"Aunt Rowena's?" Jan echoed incredulously. "What on earth are you talking about?"

There was a silence, and turning to glance at the children, Jan saw they'd both flushed scarlet.

"What do you mean, Julie?" she repeated. "I don't remember Aunt Rowena wearing any jewellery, but even if she did, it was certainly nothing like these!"

Both children remained silent, and, puzzled and irritated, Jan moved on to the next case. Now, her curiosity returned and she wondered again what the child had meant. When they were all having supper, and no interruptions were likely, she would ask again.

The train pulled into Broadminster station, and they gathered their things together and stepped out of its warmth into the freezing evening. To the children's delight, snow was still falling thickly. All the way home, they kept rushing ahead and scooping up handfuls to hurl at each other. By the time they reached Rylands, both were wet through.

"Don't worry, it will still be here in the morning," Jan told them as they went up the drive. "Now, as soon as I've turned off the alarm, straight upstairs, both of you, and into a hot bath."

Obediently they waited in the hall while she fumbled for several seconds before, realizing the alarm was not switched on, she emerged from the meter cupboard. "That's funny, it was almost the last thing Lily said before—" She broke off as the cat, ears flat against its head and tail like a bottle brush, went streaking past her and round the corner to the back hall.

"Whatever's the matter with Lotus?" Jan followed the children in pursuit of the animal, which they found cowering in the far corner of the kitchen, belly to the floor. Julie got on her hands and knees to coax it out, and Ben said suddenly, "Look— Lily's coat's still on the hook."

Jan's eyes followed his through the kitchen doorway to the coat hooks in the passage. "But it can't be—I mean, she wouldn't have gone without it."

"Perhaps she's still here, and that's why she hasn't done the alarm."

"But she'd have heard us come in. And anyway the lights weren't on."

Julie straightened and the three of them looked at each other.

Jan said, "Perhaps she's been taken ill. You two stay here while—"

"No, Mummy, please! Let us come with you!" Their frightened eyes pleaded with her as they shivered in their snow-soaked clothes.

"All right." She wanted to tell them to keep behind her, but that was tantamount to admitting she was frightened. They emerged from the kitchen in a bunch and made their way back to the main hall. Jan stood looking up the dark staircase.

"Lily?" she called, not really expecting an answer. "Are you there?"

She switched on the landing light and they went up together, looking anxiously to right and left at the top of the stairs. The corridor stretched blandly in both directions.

Jan said with false bravery, "I don't think there's anything to worry about, but we'll have a look to make sure. Let's start with my room. We'll go down to the end on this side, and back up the other."

With the children close behind her, they started their bizarre search. Her room and the spare guest-room next door were empty and undisturbed. Jan paused to draw the curtain across the window at the end of the passage, and they started up the other side. Another guest-room, Edward and Rowena's room with the *en suite* bathroom, the old nursery where Ben slept. It was there that disquiet turned to fear. Ben said in a high voice, "I didn't leave the window that wide!"

"It wasn't open at all," Jan answered. "Don't you remember, I closed it."

"But I opened it again," he whispered. "So Lotus could get in. Only a little bit—not like that."

Someone had got into the house. But if the alarm wasn't on, it must have been while Lily was still here. So where *was* Lily? A pulse was beating insistently at the base of Jan's throat. Oh God, she thought, I wish Roger was here. I wish *anybody* was here!

"We'll just finish checking the rooms, then we'll go down and phone Lily." And please let her be safely at home. Rowena had given her the number in case of emergencies.

Bathroom and lavatory revealed nothing, and Jan breathed more easily. She'd begun to wonder if Lily, feeling unwell, had collapsed in there. Julie's bedroom was as empty and undisturbed as the rest of the house. The last remaining room was Edward's study next to the stairhead. As soon as they'd looked in there, she'd phone the police.

She pushed the door open, and for several seconds her brain continued its planning. Then she lurched backwards, pulling the door shut and holding on to the handle for support. For Lily was in there, lying face down on the floor, and Jan, who had never until that week seen a dead person, knew beyond shadow of doubt that she had just seen another.

CHAPTER 7

The phone was ringing as Webb let himself into his flat.

"A murder reported in Broadminster, guv, but they reckon it's your pigeon." It was the station sergeant. "Court Lane are holding the fort, and DI Bates and Sergeant Partridge are on their way."

"Who is it, did they say?"

"The housekeeper at the Langley house."

"What was the call timed at?"

"Eighteen thirty-nine. Half an hour ago."

Webb sighed. "OK, Andy. Thanks." Just as well they'd had a decent lunch at the Printers' Ink; God knows when they'd eat again. He sighed, checked his own watch. Ken should be just about home. He dialled and Jackson's voice sounded in his ear.

"Don't take your shoes off, Ken," he said heavily. "We're off to Broadminster. The housekeeper's dead."

It was eight o'clock by the time they reached the house. An Incident caravan was in the driveway, and two police cars parked outside, along with a couple of unmarked vehicles. Across the road, several curtains twitched as the neighbours tried to assess what was going on. Snow continued to fall, fat, cold splodges of it settling on nose and eyebrows as they went up the drive. The constable on duty saluted and opened the door for them. They were met in the hall by a uniformed sergeant.

"Doc Roscoe's up there now, sir," he informed Webb.

"She's in one of the bedrooms?"

"Mr. Langley's study. Mrs. Coverdale, his sister, found her when she got back from London."

"Has Dr. Stapleton been contacted?"

"Yes, sir. He was over at Heatherton, but he's expected any minute."

"Where's Mrs. Coverdale?"

The sergeant nodded to a door on the left. "She and the kids are in the library, with WDS Lucas."

"And Inspector Bates?"

The man hesitated. "I'm not sure, sir. He came downstairs, but he might have gone back up."

"Are Scenes of Crime here?"

"Yes, they're upstairs."

Webb nodded and started up the stairs, glancing admiringly at the handsome stained-glass window. The police surgeon was at the top of the stairs, talking to Dick Hodges. Don Partridge hovered behind them.

"Ah, Chief Inspector. We've met before, I believe. Roscoe's the name."

"That's right, doctor—the Delilah case. You've confirmed death?"

He nodded. "It was only a cursory examination, so I can't tell you much; but I'd say the cause was a blow to the back of the head."

"Any idea of time?"

"Hard to say, in a centrally heated house. Probably six or eight hours. Mrs. Coverdale says she left the house at ten."

"Entry seems to have been through the room on the far left," Hodges volunteered. "Window open, and flat roof below."

Webb turned, scanning the men in the corridor. "Where's Inspector Bates?" he asked Partridge.

"He went downstairs, guv—wanted to take a look outside."

"See if you can find him, will you? I want to know what Mrs. Coverdale told him before I see her."

Partridge ran back down the stairs and Webb moved to the open door immediately on the right. A photographer stood just inside and Webb waited till he moved to a different angle before stepping inside.

It was a small room—barely ten feet square—and the woman was lying face down in the middle of it, her head towards the door. Dark, ugly stains matted the grey hair and smeared the heavy glass ashtray lying beside her. Webb registered every detail, then, with practised detachment, turned his attention to her surroundings.

Along the left-hand wall, bookshelves and filing cabinets had been emptied and their contents littered the floor. The drawers of a desk beneath the window were open, and on the wall, a set of magnificent photographs of mountain peaks had been pushed askew. There was little space to move, and he decided to leave a more detailed inspection till the SOCOs had finished.

He rejoined the group on the landing in time to see Partridge rushing up the stairs two at a time. "It's the DI, guv!" he gasped, catching sight of Webb. "He's lying out there in the snow, and he's not moving!"

Webb pushed the nearest man out of his way and started down the stairs, aware of the doctor, Jackson and Partridge close behind him. The front door stood open, with the startled constable beside it, staring up at them.

"Round the side of the house," Partridge directed between gasps. The cold air seized their breath, and the snow almost blinded them. Webb could feel his shoes sinking deep into it as he ran, and cursed himself for not having stopped to put on his boots. A black shape was lying sprawled at the back corner of the house, with the uniformed sergeant kneeling beside it. He looked up as they arrived.

"There is a pulse, but it's pretty faint."

"How long has he been out here?" Webb snapped, as the doctor took charge.

"I don't know, guv." It was Partridge who answered. "Not long before you arrived—ten minutes at most."

"You didn't hear any sounds? A shot or anything?"

The man shook his head, his startled eyes meeting Webb's.

"Radio for an ambulance," the doctor said over his shoulder. "We can't get him to a car without a stretcher."

"What is it, Doc?" Webb asked urgently. "Has he been attacked?"

"It's hard to tell." The sergeant was already using his pocket radio. "The Royal Broadshire's only just down the road. In the meantime, get some rugs and blankets, and something to keep the snow off him."

The two sergeants went stumbling back across the snow and Webb said tensely, "How bad is he?"

"Not good. We'll know more when we can examine him properly. I've finished upstairs, so I'll go with him. There's nothing you can do."

But Webb still hesitated, his anxiety underlaid by a feeling of guilt. He hadn't particularly liked Bates, had been abrupt with him this last week. Now, he'd be glad of the chance to make amends.

The sergeants came floundering back, laden with blankets pulled off one of the beds. As they were draped round the prone body, Partridge put up a large black umbrella and held it over the group on the ground. Suddenly, in the cold silence, came the welcome wail of a siren, and minutes later blue, flashing lights could be seen at the gate.

"We'll leave you to it, then," Webb said gruffly. "You'll keep me informed?"

"Of course."

With an effort he wrenched his mind off the injured man and returned to more immediate duties. "I want the grounds searched immediately. It seems unlikely any attacker would be hanging about in this weather, but we have to make sure. Tracks in the snow might help, but it's coming down so hard they wouldn't last more than a few minutes. I'll send out some reinforcements. In the meantime, Sergeant Jackson, we'll have a word with Mrs. Coverdale. No knowing, now, what she told Inspector Bates."

Had that information led to an attack? Back in the warm house, he crisply detailed more men to join in the search. Then he tapped on the library door and went inside. The woman detective rose to her feet, but Janis Coverdale and her children, huddled together on the sofa, simply looked up at him mutely.

"Detective-Sergeant Lucas, sir."

"I remember you, Miss Lucas. I noticed the Incident caravan

outside; would you be kind enough to organize coffee and sandwiches all round?"

Jan said automatically, "Could the children have milk, please?"

Mary Lucas nodded and left the room. Webb would have preferred not to have them there at all, but there was no way they would leave their mother at the moment. The little boy, pale beneath his fading tan, asked anxiously, "Is Lily really dead?"

"I'm afraid so, sonny."

"Then it's my fault!" The child looked stricken, and Webb raised his eyebrows at the woman.

"Ben left his window open, because the cat was outside. It had been pushed farther up, so presumably—"

"You can't blame yourself, Ben," Webb said gently. "If someone was set on getting in, he'd soon have broken a window."

"There's an alarm," Jan said. "Lily would have put it on before she left."

"I'm sure she would." She was as much in need of reassurance as the children. "Now, I know this is painful for you, Mrs. Coverdale, but I'd like you to tell me exactly what happened when you got back from London."

She looked bewildered. "But I've been through it all with Inspector Bates."

"He's—been called away," Webb said. No point in adding to her alarm. "If you wouldn't mind telling me."

This particular result of murder hadn't occurred to her before, the endless repetition of it all, with everyone needing to be told the same story over and over. That's how it had been last time, with the other body. God, how many of them was she to be called upon to see?

Fighting down imminent hysteria, she forced herself to meet Webb's eyes and their calm, patient gaze steadied her. Slowly and carefully, omitting nothing, she repeated her story.

"And Mrs.—I'm sorry, I don't know her name?"

Jan stared at him, her hand to her mouth. "How *awful!* Neither do I! Rowena never mentioned it."

"Don't worry, we'll find out. Lily, then. She didn't say how long she'd be here?"

"No, just that she'd one or two things to finish."

"And she didn't seem worried or on edge?"

"Not at all."

Mary Lucas came back with a tray. Jan realized, with a sense of guilt, that she was ravenously hungry. She watched with a growing sense of detachment as the woman officer set out food and drink and quietly left the room.

It was bizarre, unreal, to be eating sandwiches with the detectives, while Lily lay upstairs with her head bashed in. With an intensity that disturbed her, Jan longed to be taken in someone's arms and held very closely, as she had held the children. But Roger was twelve thousand miles away, and no longer cared for her anyway.

Sensing that her control was faltering, Webb said, "The Scenes of Crime officers will be here for some time, Mrs. Coverdale. Is there anywhere you and the children could go?"

"I'm sure Lady Peel would have us—my brother's mother-in-law." So she needn't sleep in this house after all. Oh, thank God!

A knock on the door interrupted them, and one of the police officers put his head round the door.

"Telephone for you, sir."

Bates! Webb hurried to the phone in the hall. "Yes?"

"Roscoe here, Chief Inspector. There's no need to look for an assailant; your man's suffering from a perforated ulcer."

"Good God! Is he all right?"

"It's a messy one. He's still in the operating theatre."

"But he will make it?"

"Stands a fair chance. Any idea of his next of kin?"

Shame flooded over Webb. He'd never bothered to inquire. Come to think of it, he'd never had any kind of personal conversation with Stan.

"I can find out."

"Better get on to them."

Webb depressed the receiver rest, lifted his hand and dialled again, leaving instructions with Carrington Street. Then he turned to the constable on the door.

"Call off the search, would you? It was a false alarm."

What bloody timing! he thought, as he went back to the library. But the man hadn't been well since he joined them; all those pills he'd kept taking.

Jackson looked up quickly as he entered the room. Webb gave him a quick nod. Ken would have to wonder a bit longer; he didn't want to add more drama to the interview.

"Now, Mrs. Coverdale, will you cast your mind back to before Christmas—the eighteenth of December, in fact. Can you remember how you spent the day?"

"As it happens, I can. It was our first day here."

"Was your brother at home?"

"No, he was making the final arrangements for his trip."

"Here, or in London?"

"I'm not sure. Is it important?"

"It could be." So it was technically possible for Langley to have murdered Marriott. But since there was no doubt he'd left the country—Passport Control having confirmed it—he couldn't have killed his housekeeper.

Webb nodded towards a photograph on the bureau. "Is that him?"

"It's their wedding photo, yes."

He walked over and studied it with interest. Though the face of a younger man, it wouldn't have changed that much; and there was indeed a resemblance to Marriott in the broad, slightly protuberant forehead, the low-growing hair and deep-set eyes. Webb wondered again how significant that similarity was.

He said, "Have you heard from him since he left?"

"No, but I wouldn't expect to. There's no postal service in the jungle."

"So there's no way of contacting him?"

"Do you need to?" Alarm sounded in her voice. "Why?"

"Because," he said gently, "this is the second death directly connected with him. The wallet could have been a coincidence, but not this."

She stared at him, her blue eyes brilliant with fear, and the little girl, sensing her mother's tension, pressed closer against her and began to whimper. There was another knock on the door.

"Excuse me, sir, the Chief Constable and Detective Chief Superintendant Fleming have arrived."

He'd been expecting the top brass. In the light of a second murder, police authority would have to be in evidence.

"I'll be with you in a moment, Constable." He turned back to the woman. "I must report to my senior officers, Mrs. Coverdale, but I still have some questions for you. Miss Lucas will drive you round to—Lady Peel, did you say?" (As if he'd not enough on his plate, without a bloody handle to contend with.) "Then, in a couple of hours or so, when you've had time to settle in and the children are in bed, we can resume our talk."

Chief Constable Sir Frederick Arthur Soames was, Jackson thought, very much as one would expect him to be. Which is to say he was tall, stout, and prosperous-looking, his size now emphasized still further by a cashmere overcoat with beaver collar. Beneath it, Jackson caught sight of a bow tie, which explained his late arrival. An interrupted function, no doubt. He had a protruding stomach, a couple of chins, and a pale and piercing eye. Beside him, the Detective Super looked as small and dapper as a sparrow, but Jackson knew Fleming and was more comfortable with him. Not, thank goodness, that either of them took any notice of him. He watched sympathetically as Webb went with them into the now empty library.

"Devil of it is, Webb," the Chief Constable was rumbling, "the connections of this particular family. No chance of playing it down. The press were arriving in droves as we came in. Damn it, I used to play golf with Reggie Peel, and his daughter's married to Langley."

"Yes, sir."

"Was anything taken, Spider?" Fleming cut in.

"We've no way of knowing, sir. Mrs. Coverdale isn't familiar with the house any longer, so the only person who could have told us is the victim. The silver hasn't been touched, though."

"Since she was found in the study, she must have caught him in there. In which case, it wasn't silver he was after."

"Then what, Phil? Have you anything in mind?"

"Nothing specific, sir. But since we must assume these deaths are connected, perhaps he was looking for whatever he'd hoped to find in the wallet."

"By George, that's a thought," said the Chief Constable admiringly.

"So what does one keep in a wallet or desk drawer? Money and credit cards aren't the answer—the killer left them with the body. Driving licence? Hardly. Safe-deposit box numbers, valuable stamps? Private papers of some kind?"

Webb said, "I've a strong feeling that whatever it is, is related to Mr. Langley being an explorer. The bandage on the first body is a pointer. Both Mrs. Coverdale and Mr. Coady thought so." He explained the mummy theory, while the senior men listened attentively.

"There were also some sequins. Any ideas on those?"

Webb shrugged. "Jewels? It's all I can think of. The trouble is, it's a three-sided case—Langley, Marriott, the killer. So far we haven't established any connection between them. Still, we should be receiving copies of Marriott's papers tomorrow. There may be something in them which links him to Mr. Langley."

"What we need," said the Chief Constable crisply, "is something linking him with his killer. In the meantime, we'll stop pussy-footing about and get the lab boys to turn this place over. If they can find what the murderer was looking for, we might get somewhere. Now you'd better go and placate those newsmen outside. They've got a personal stake in this, remember."

"A press conference is already arranged, sir, for the morning. They know that."

"But we now have not one body, but two."

The Chief Constable had a distressing habit of stating the

obvious. "Indeed, sir," Webb agreed blandly, and caught Fleming's sharp-eyed glance. He got to his feet. "If you'll excuse me, then, I'll go and have a word with them. As you say, they won't like hanging round in this weather."

The past two hours had been a continuing nightmare. Lady Peel's voice on the phone, faint with shock—though she'd been able to supply Lily's surname, Carr—and the police handing down their nightclothes because, suddenly, they couldn't go upstairs; and the ride to Cajabamba in the police car, with Lotus loudly yowling her protests from her lidded basket on Ben's knee.

The children, though dropping with weariness after their long day, had been difficult to settle in the strange surroundings, and finally Lady Peel offered to read them a story. "About Peru!" they'd pleaded, in need of the comfort of familiar ritual, though Peru was the last thing Jan wanted to think about, reminding her as it did of Edward and his possible rôle in what had happened.

And now here she was, by the resurrected fire in Lady Peel's drawing-room, with the still-nervous cat on her lap, and the policemen, their own faces drawn with tiredness, sipping at yet more coffee and awaiting her cooperation.

She attempted a smile. "How can I help you, Mr. Webb?"

He put down his coffee-cup. "It's possible your brother's occupation has a bearing on the case—the mummy, perhaps also the sequins. Is there anything valuable that he could have brought back with him, which someone might want to get his hands on?"

"I doubt it. Inca graves have been plundered for hundreds of years—there's no chance of finding a Tutankhamen's tomb. Even when my father discovered Cajabamba, it was the temple and shrines and the architecture generally which were important."

"And what exactly is Cajabamba?"

She smiled. "I'm sorry—I'm so steeped in it all, I forget everyone else isn't. It was a 'lost city' of the Incas. People knew of its existence, but not its location. Several expeditions set out to look for it, and the one my father went on with Laurence Coady and Reginald Peel discovered it. The jungle growth had almost completely buried it."

Hannah had mentioned that. "When was this, Mrs. Coverdale?"

"In nineteen-fifty. It was the second of three they went on together. My father wrote a book about it, *The Hidden City*, which became a best-seller."

"So he was a writer as well as an explorer."

She smiled. "He could do anything he put his mind to. Before the war, he was a lecturer in Spanish at Oxford."

"Then he joined the services, I suppose?"

"Till he was invalided out, in forty-two. After that, he went into counter-intelligence."

Webb raised an eyebrow. "Academic, spy-catcher, explorer and writer. He was certainly versatile. At what stage did your brother start going with him?"

"He never did. Edward only became interested after his marriage, because Rowena was so keen. She'd been accompanying her father since she was seventeen."

"But didn't your father go with them?"

"No, he only went those three times."

"And Laurence Coady?"

"Oh, he'd been visiting Peru for years—it was he who persuaded the others. But after fifty-five, he never went back, either. Only Sir Reginald did, with Rowena when she was old enough, then with both her and Edward."

"But isn't that rather strange? Why did the other two drop out?"

"I don't know," Jan said slowly. "It's something I've thought about recently. Admittedly, that third expedition was traumatic for my father. He caught some virulent disease and was in hospital in Lima almost the whole trip. But after some ups and downs, the other two achieved their objective."

"And what was that?"

"To trace Manco Inca's surviving descendant."

Webb forebore from asking who Manco Inca was. "Am I right in assuming this is Sir Reginald's house?" Jan nodded. "And he died only recently, I believe?"

"Last October, yes."

"Last October," repeated Webb thoughtfully. And the wallets had been stolen on the first of November. His mind went back over what she had told him. "Was it pure coincidence that all three men lived in Broadminster?"

"I'd wondered about that, too, and asked Lady Peel. She said they and the Coadys moved down to be near my father, to make for easier planning."

"When was that?"

Jan paused. Then she said slowly, "After the third expedition."

"So there *wasn't* any more planning, not with all three of them?"

"No."

"That third expedition had long-lasting consequences. I wonder what really happened on it."

Jan looked down at the sleeping cat, gently caressing its silken brown ears. The Chief Inspector had put into words her own doubts, which everyone else she'd questioned had discounted. But surely nothing that had happened over thirty years ago could have caused these two recent deaths?

Wanting to dispel his doubts as well as her own, she began, "But surely—" and broke off as a shrill scream rang through the house. She leapt to her feet, spilling the startled cat onto the rug, and rushed to the door with the two policemen behind her. This terrible, endless day was still not over.

CHAPTER 8

The noise was coming from the children's room. As Jan reached the top of the stairs, she met Lady Peel in her dressing-gown, a plait of grey hair over one shoulder, hurrying along the passage.

"Whatever is it?" she quavered, a hand to her throat. Without stopping to answer, Jan pushed open the bedroom door. Julie was sitting up in bed, still screaming, and Ben, pale with shock, was shaking her by the arm and shouting at her.

The sudden acute relief made Jan go limp. A nightmare—only a nightmare, and hardly surprising. Having assured himself it was nothing serious, Webb said quietly, "We'll wait downstairs." Lady Peel, too, had melted away.

Jan hurried to the bed, catching the shaking child in her arms. "Hush, darling, Mummy's here. It was only a dream."

"But it *wasn't!*" Julie's pyjamas were damp with sweat. "I *saw* her! In the wardrobe, with the jewels!"

"The wardrobe?" Jan looked in bewilderment at the old oak cupboard against the wall.

"Ben saw her too!"

"Don't be stupid!" Ben said quickly. "How could I see your dream?"

"She tried to pull me inside!" Julie collapsed against her mother, sobbing hysterically.

"She's talking rubbish!" There was relief in Ben's voice.

Jan stroked the damp hair soothingly. "Tell me about it, then. It will make the badness go away."

"No, don't!" Ben's voice was a shout. Seeing her surprise, he added more quietly, "*I* don't want to have nightmares."

"But if she describes it, she'll see how silly it is. Dreams are frightening when we're half asleep, because then, anything seems possible. If you look at them when you're awake, you know there's no way they can be true."

"But I wasn't asleep," Julie said against her chest. "Not the first time."

"You've dreamt this before?"

"Shut *up*, Julie!" Ben said fiercely. "It's OK, now just shut up!"

Julie raised her head, meeting his warning gaze. Jan felt a tremor go through her, then she freed herself from her mother's arms. "I'm all right," she said unconvincingly.

Jan looked from one to the other of them, but they avoided her eyes. "It's all the upset, darling, that made you dream, and the Crown Jewels got jumbled up in your mind and became part of it. There's nothing to be frightened about."

Julie nodded, lying back on her pillow, and after a minute Ben climbed into his own bed.

"All right now?"

They both nodded.

"Lady Peel and I are here, and the policemen too. You're quite safe, so go back to sleep."

But the mention of jewels reminded her that she'd meant to question Julie about her remark at the Tower.

"All well?" Webb asked, when she reached the drawing-room.

"I think so."

"As it's after midnight, we'll be on our way and let you get some sleep. We'll be in touch later."

So they still hadn't finished with her. Jan forced her tired brain to practicalities. "When can we go back to Rylands?"

"It'll be several days, I'm afraid. The Chief Constable's calling in the lab, and they'll be going over the whole house."

"But all our things are there!"

"We'll get out what we can, once it's been cleared."

And with that, she had to be content. Wearily she locked up after the policemen and went at last to bed.

Bates's empty desk the next morning was a guilty reminder. Webb pulled his phone across and dialled the hospital. The patient had had a comfortable night—that was as much as he could glean. But he'd be down for the PM this afternoon, and would look in then. His conscience slightly appeased, he turned to the bulky packet on his desk. It contained photocopies of the documents taken from Marriott's flat, together with a transcription of the shorthand pads.

Skipping through the latter, with their racy colloquial style, the man began to come alive for him, but as expected, there was nothing relating to December. Dates on various sets of notes were given as October and November. No doubt the killer had destroyed the December pad. Webb put them on one side and turned to the diary. And it was then that a name leapt out of the page. He reached for the phone.

"Ken? In here, at the double, and bring your notes on the wallet owners."

Jackson arrived, breathless, within seconds. "On to something, guv?"

"We could be. Can you find the interview with Rollo?"

"Right—got it."

"What did he say when we asked about Marriott?"

"Question: 'Have you ever come across a man called Guy Marriott?' Reply: 'Sorry, never heard of him.' "

"As I thought. He wasn't telling the truth. Look at this."

Jackson came round the desk and bent over Webb's shoulder. The diary page was open at the week beginning 3rd November, and under Thursday 6th was scribbled "The Commodore: A. J. Rollo 12:15—4 P.M."

Jackson gave a low whistle. "Reckon it's the same chap?"

"Not that many people called Rollo. What was his full name?"

"Anthony James."

"There you are. Funny the duration of the appointment being noted. I wonder if it's significant—and what Mr. Rollo was up to yesterday." He glanced at his watch. "The press conference is almost due. Once that's over, we'll detail actions from the diary and address book, then back to Broadminster for the PM. Too bad Stan's laid up—we're under pressure now, and a man short."

"Telephone for Mrs. Coverdale, my lady." The uniformed maid
—Jan couldn't remember her name—stood in the doorway.
They were in the drawing-room, which to Jan still wore its
persona of the previous night, with the policemen's questions
heavy on the air. The games table had been set up, but so far the
children hadn't looked at it. They were heavy-eyed and subdued, Julie in particular following Jan like a puppy every time
she left the room.

"For me?" It could only be the police, she thought with a
feeling of dread, following the maid to where the instrument,
laid on polished wood, awaited her. But the voice that greeted
her was, if anything, even less welcome.

"Janis? Thank God I've found you! What on earth is going
on?"

It was Roger's mother. "Hello, Dora," she said flatly.

"I tried to ring you yesterday, but the woman who answered
said you'd gone to London. Then this morning, I heard on the
news—"

"What time did you phone?" Jan interrupted urgently, only
as the words were spoken reflecting wryly that she was beginning to think like the police.

"What? Oh, I don't know. About lunch-time, I suppose.
Why?" Horror crept into her voice. "You don't mean it was—
that I actually spoke to—Oh, my God!"

"Please try to think, Dora. It might be important."

"Well, it wasn't till I got back from the shops that I looked at
the paper, and read about that body being mistaken for Edward.
The main surprise was that it was you who identified it. Or
didn't, if you see what I mean. I'd no idea you were over. Why
on earth didn't you tell us you were coming? Are Roger and the
children with you?"

It was just like Roger to put off telling his parents, Jan thought
resignedly. Julie had crept up behind her, and she reached out
an arm and drew her close.

"Roger and I have separated," she said quietly. "I'm sorry
you hadn't heard."

There was a brief pause. Then: "You're not serious, surely?"

"Very serious."

"But you were always so happy! Whatever happened?"

Jan looked down at Julie, noting with concern that she was sucking her thumb, a habit broken more than two years ago. "I can't go into it now, Dora. I'll explain when I see you."

"But that's why I'm phoning—when *will* we see you? You'd better come straight over—you can't stay there, with people being killed all the time!"

"We're with Lady Peel, and we're—quite safe." She prayed the tremor in her voice hadn't reached Julie. "The police need me here at the moment, but we'll come as soon as we can."

"At least send the children to us. They shouldn't be exposed to all that."

"But they don't know you, Dora. It's kind of you, but they need to be with me."

Mrs. Coverdale said stiffly, "Very well, if you think that's best. And where's Roger, while all this is going on?"

"In Sydney."

"All by himself at home?"

"Not at home, and not by himself."

"You're not saying *he*— I mean, since you're over here, I assumed—"

"It was he who left, Dora."

There was a silence, and when Dora Coverdale spoke again, her voice was unsteady. "This is terrible. I just can't take it in. Still, I realize we can't discuss it now. Please do remember, though, that we're your family too. Don't cut us off, just because Roger—"

"Of course I won't."

"We're longing to see you, and our grandchildren. Now more than ever. As soon as you can get away, just give us a ring."

"I will, Dora. And—thank you."

Jan turned from the phone, fighting down tears. Julie slipped her hand with its wet thumb inside her mother's. "What did Granny Dora want?"

"Just to give us her love." She ought to tell Mr. Webb about that phone call, but he'd said he'd be contacting her. It could wait till then.

Miles arrived half an hour later. Lady Peel had phoned him after breakfast.

"Two bodies in three days!" he commented. "Do the police think they're connected?"

"Edward seems to be the link," Jan said unwillingly.

"But why poor, harmless Lily?"

"Because she took him by surprise," Lady Peel said briskly. "She'd have come across him searching the house, so he killed her in a panic—he mightn't even have meant to."

"But it wasn't just a burglary that went wrong," Jan objected. "No casual thief would have gone to the study. He'd have taken the TV or video or something."

"A point," Miles conceded. "So what do you think he was looking for?"

"Perhaps something he'd expected Mr. Marriott to have. Though what the connection is with Edward—"

"If you're assuming it's the same killer," Lady Peel broke in, "I have to disagree. Lily's death is a tragedy, but in these violent times, not unusual. The first murder was quite different. The killer was playing games, dressing up the body and so on. There was even a touch of macabre humour with the sequins. But there's nothing remotely amusing about knocking an elderly woman on the head."

"In an emergency," Miles said drily, "he wouldn't have time to be inventive. Still"—with a glance at the children, seated at the games table but possibly within earshot—"enough of death and disaster. May I lighten the proceedings by suggesting a day out tomorrow? You too, Mary, if you'd care to join us. The wildfowl trust is open all year—the children might like to go there. We could round the day off with supper at Clarence Mews —a take-away or something. It would at least give you a day away from it all."

Miles's willingness to endure the children's company surprised Jan, and she was touched by the measure of his concern.

"That's a very kind thought," she said warmly, "we'd be delighted."

"Forgive me if I don't join you," Lady Peel murmured. "This cold weather is a trial, and I'm happier by my own fire. But by all means go out and enjoy yourselves. Heaven knows, you've earned a respite."

Dr. Stapleton, who was based at the Royal Broadshire, again conducted the post mortem, and this time there were no surprises. Death was caused by a blow to the back of the head, consistent with being hit with the heavy, sharp-edged ashtray which had been found at the scene. Tests would almost certainly match the blood on it to that of the dead woman. Time of death would be established after analysis of the stomach contents, but was most likely between midday and 2 p.m.

"Lunch-time," Webb said gloomily. "Not easy to check alibis during lunch-time." He thought again of the bank-manager, who lunched at the Commodore Hotel. When he'd been to the hospital, they'd pay him another visit.

Bates was lying propped up on pillows, with a sinister assortment of tubes disappearing under the bedclothes. He opened his eyes as Webb approached with the requisite bunch of grapes, and automatically struggled to straighten himself, stopping with a grimace of pain.

"I'm sorry, skipper!" he began, before Webb could speak. "What an infernal thing to happen, right in the middle of a case!"

"By the look of you, that's the least of your worries. I'm not denying we could use you, but we're just about coping." He seated himself gingerly on the chair beside the bed. "The important thing is, how are you feeling?"

"Not too good, to be honest, but it'll be better once the poison drains away. Never mind all that, how's the case going?"

Absolved from further solicitous inquiry, Webb gladly changed the subject and brought him up to date on developments. "I don't mind telling you, you put the wind up us!" he added with a grin. "We thought you'd been attacked while inspecting the grounds. Got a search underway—hopeless, really, in all that snow. Then Doc Roscoe phoned and put us in the picture."

Bates smiled weakly. He seemed to be tiring, and Webb wondered if he should go. But then he said, "So now you're off to see this Rollo chap again?"

"That's right—he's got a bit of explaining to do. Oh, and we had a response to that picture you organized. Café-owner down here recognized Marriott. Said he'd been in for lunch before Christmas, so we want a word with him, too."

"Too bad I can't do my stint. I'm no use to anyone, cooped up here."

"Don't worry about it; just concentrate on getting better." He paused. "Family been in?"

"The wife and son, yes." Bates gave a faint smile. "At least it's nearer for them to come here than if I'd been in Shillingham. Might as well look on the bright side."

"You live actually in Heatherton?"

"Just this side of it. Twenty minutes' drive." He hesitated. "Will they get you another replacement, skip?"

"I don't know, Stan. Depends how long you're likely to be laid up. Alan Crombie's away three months."

"Sorry to let you down like this."

"Don't be daft," Webb said gruffly. "I must be on my way now, but I'll look in again and keep you posted. Take care, and don't do anything I wouldn't do."

The last time he'd been in a hospital, he reflected, walking back along the shiny corridors that smelled of disinfectant, was when he'd called in with Jackson to visit Millie and the twins. Once this case was over, he must go round to see his godson.

The café-owner was willing to help but had little to offer. He was at least certain of the date, since it was the day he put up his Christmas tree, and Marriott had commented on it. "Never do it till a week before Christmas," he explained, "and down it comes straight after New Year. Can't be bothered with all the clutter, to be honest, but the customers seem to expect it."

"He didn't say where he was going, or ask for directions?"

"Fraid not, sir. He just passed the time of day, like, then got on with his omelet and chips. I did ask, when he mentioned Christmas, if he'd got any kiddies, and he laughed and said, 'Not on your life.' "

"You say he arrived just after two. How long was he here?"

The man shrugged. "About an hour. The rush was over, so we didn't need his table. When he'd finished his meal, he got out a pad and spent some time writing. And he had two cups of coffee. Seemed to be filling in time, probably till he had to meet someone."

"So he left here about three?"

"That's right, mate, give or take a few minutes. Poor bloke, I little thought he was going out to his death. Gave me quite a turn, seeing his picture in the *News.*"

Webb unfolded a street map and spread it on the countertop. The Golden Pear was in the High Street, not far from where Marriott had left his car. Presumably it was on his route, but that left open three-quarters of Broadminster.

"Well, thanks for your help, Mr. Brown." Webb made a play of patting his pocket. "Must get myself some cash before the banks close. Have you a branch of the National nearby?"

"Yes, mate. Other side of the road, just past the Market Street turning. You can't miss it."

"Thank you." So that could easily have been Marriott's destination. Turning up their collars, they went out into the snow.

Mr. Rollo was not pleased to see them. He showed them into his office with controlled impatience and said curtly, "I've already helped you all I can, gentlemen, and I have an interview with a client in five minutes."

Webb watched him as he shuffled papers on his desk. He had a heavy face, early good looks having coarsened to the blurred outlines of middle-age. There were incipient bags under the dark eyes, and the black, un-English hair was sprinkled with grey.

"We won't detain you longer than necessary, sir," Webb said smoothly, "but we have a point to clear up. When we saw you on Tuesday, you assured us you hadn't heard of Guy Marriott."

"Well?"

"Well, sir, we have reason to believe that wasn't the truth."

The man's sallow face flushed. "I'm not used to being called a liar, Officer," he said stiffly.

"You still maintain you didn't know the gentleman?"

"Of course I do."

"Could you tell me then, sir, what you were doing on"—he made an unnecessary reference to the notebook in his hand—"Thursday, 6th November?"

"Good God, that's more than two months ago. Without consulting my diary, I've no idea."

"Perhaps I can help you, sir. You had lunch at the Commodore Hotel in London. With Mr. Marriott."

The man stared at him and little beads of sweat broke out on his forehead. Webb sat in silence, waiting.

"I do go to London occasionally," Rollo said at last. "And I may well have lunched at the Commodore. But not, I assure you, with Mr. Marriott. As I told you, we never met."

Webb's face remained impassive, but he was puzzled. Something about that lunch engagement caused the man acute anxiety, yet his voice, when he denied all knowledge of Marriott, had the ring of truth.

"Perhaps you'd tell us, then, who you did meet?"

Again that flash, deep in the dark eyes—of wariness? Fear? "It was a business engagement."

"Ah, so you *do* remember?"

Rollo said drily, "It's coming back to me," and Webb felt a grudging admiration. Seeing that a name was awaited, the man added reluctantly, "I believe that was the day I lunched with Mr. Roy Sinclair, of Lee Charterhouse."

"The stock-brokers?"

Rollo swallowed nervously. "That's right. We first met at a financial conference a couple of years back."

"You must have had a lot to talk about."

"I beg your pardon?"

"It was a long lunch, wasn't it? Twelve-fifteen till four o'clock?"

The heightened colour drained away, leaving Rollo's skin even more sallow and emphasizing his Italian ancestry. With an effort, he said, "We'd some business to discuss."

"I see. And where were you at lunch-time yesterday?"

The man looked at him blankly. His mind was obviously still on the previous question. "Yesterday? I was here, of course."

"Surely you went out to eat?"

"Oh—yes. I go home for lunch, Chief Inspector. As you know, I live close by."

As Webb had remarked, lunches were notoriously hard to verify. And Mrs. Rollo, if appealed to, would back her husband, whether he were there or no.

The phone sounded on the desk. Rollo put out a hand and flicked a switch.

"Mrs. Brewster's here, Mr. Rollo."

"Thank you. Tell her I shan't keep her a moment." He sat staring down at the phone, then wrenched his eyes back to Webb. "Is that all you need to know?"

Webb returned his gaze, and it was the bank-manager's eyes which fell first. "For the moment, Mr. Rollo, but we know where to find you."

Outside, a blueness was seeping into the afternoon and it was freezing hard. "What do you make of all that, Ken?" Webb asked, turning back towards the car.

"Beats me, guv. You think he really didn't know Marriott?"

"It rather looks like it."

"But Marriott knew *him*. It's in his diary. Though why he should make a note about two other people meeting for lunch is beyond me—not to mention how long it went on."

"Marriott was an investigative journalist," Webb said drily, "and as you know, Ken, they move in mysterious ways. Still, we have his notebooks for November—they may give us a clue. If Rollo was up to some private hanky-panky, it's no skin off our nose. All that concerns us is whether he was connected with Marriott's death. If he wasn't, he's welcome to take all day over his lunches."

Jan had persuaded the children to play outside that afternoon, and for an hour or so, making their first snowman, they'd forgotten the cloud that hung over them. They had come in rosy and bright-eyed, and it wasn't till bedtime that a measure of fear returned. Julie, having had the first bath, was first into bed, and when Jan sat down to wait for Ben, she reached for her mother's hand.

"What is it, darling?"

"He wouldn't really try to kill us, would he, Mummy? The man who killed Lily?"

"Julie! How could you even think such a thing?"

"Ben said he would, if he found out we knew."

"Then Ben had no right to frighten you." She paused. "Knew what?"

Julie glanced at the door, but it remained half shut. "Where it is," she said in a whisper.

Jan frowned. "Where what is?"

Belated caution flushed the child's cheeks, but since her mother was waiting, she reluctantly answered, "What he'd come for."

"But he couldn't 'find out,' because you *don't* know, do you? So there's nothing to worry about."

"But if we *did?*" Julie persisted, her fingers gripping Jan's hand. *"Then* would he?"

"Darling, stop worrying! There's nothing to be frightened of, I promise."

The child started to say something, but broke off as Ben came into the room. It wasn't the time to chastise him, but she'd have a word with him tomorrow about frightening his sister. Jan kissed them both good night, and went downstairs.

"Could you lend me something to read?" she asked Lady Peel, when it was time for them, too, to go to bed. "I was browsing through a book on Peru, but I left it at Rylands."

Lady Peel smiled. "If you want another, there's plenty of choice. Reggie's books are all as he left them, in his study."

"May I borrow one? I'd take great care of it."

"My dear, help yourself."

Sir Reginald's study, unlike Edward's, was on the ground floor, a large, oak-lined room with heavy leather furniture and books all round the walls. One entire section was devoted to Peru, and Jan, spoilt for choice, almost abandoned the daunting rows of shelves for another subject. But after flicking through one or two volumes, she finally selected *Treasures of the Incas.* If, after all, she felt too tired to read, she could at least look at the colour plates.

By the time she was ready for bed, however, she was too drowsy even for pictures. Deciding to leave the book till the next day, she was laying it on the table, when she noticed a slip of paper barely visible between the leaves. Curious, she picked the book up again, opening it at the marked page.

"It is a cause of frustration to chroniclers," she read, "that two of the Incas' greatest treasures have never been found. More priceless than any that were seized by the Spaniards, they were removed from Cuzco by Manco Inca when he fled to Vilcabamba, and despite diligent searches over the centuries, have never been recovered.

"The first of these objects was the Punchao, the original golden image of the sun, which contained a powder made from the hearts of dead Incas. It was thought at one time that the Spaniards had captured this, but it later proved to be only a copy, of which many were found.

"The image was said to be surrounded by golden medallions so arranged that, when struck by the sun, they dazzled the beholder, ensuring that no one could look on the idol itself.

"The second prize to elude capture was the legendary emerald collar belonging to Cura Ocllo, wife of Manco Inca. This magnificent piece was described in detail by Juan Pizarro, younger brother of the Governor, who met his death at the hands of Manco Inca and his supporters during the siege of Cuzco in May 1536. He claimed that the nine unflawed emeralds were as large as quails' eggs and mounted on intricate gold filigree. It was reputed to be the crowning achievement of Inca craftsmen."

Jan frowned, lifting the book closer to the light. She was not mistaken; a light pencil bracket had been drawn in the margin, taking in the whole page, and alongside it was a large exclamation mark.

CHAPTER 9

"Tony! I asked if you wanted more toast?" Angela Rollo gazed at her husband in exasperation. "Honestly, I don't know what's got into you. Ever since you came home yesterday, you've been acting like a zombie—I don't think you've heard a word I've said!"

He roused himself with an effort, said automatically, "I'm sorry, dear."

"Well, do you or don't you?"

"Do I what?"

"Want some more toast, for God's sake!"

"Oh—no, thank you." He looked with faint surprise at the crumbs on his plate. He'd no recollection of eating. God, she was right—he must pull himself together. But how the *hell* had the police got on to the Commodore business? And what, in the name of heaven, did it have to do with that disreputable tramp they'd found?

Roy had assured him there was no risk. Because it wasn't only the Commodore and Camilla, though in all conscience that was bad enough. Far more potentially damaging was the link with the Bank. That, if questions were asked, could cost him his career. Might even, he thought in growing panic, land him in prison. How could he ever have been so stupid, so criminally reckless, as to have become involved?

In the large house across town, Lady Peel was also having an uncomfortable breakfast. Not in the material sense; she was, as always, propped up in the large bed, with soft pillows at her back and merino blankets over her thin legs. The room, luxuriously feminine, had its usual morning scent of toast and China tea, and the air, even at so early an hour and with snow on the outside sill, was comfortingly warm. Despite the efficiency of the central heating, she had retained her bedroom fireplace, and in this exceptionally cold weather, an open fire, safe behind its guard, burned day and night.

But like Rollo at his kitchen table, her mind was not on the meal. For the double murder, terrible enough in itself, seemed to her the embodiment of a disquiet she had lived with for thirty years. Her greatest fear, now, was that the police would uncover a trail leading back not only to Edward, but to dear Reggie. And how could she bear that?

Strange, she reflected, sipping the almost colourless tea, that Janis should have asked about that expedition. Or perhaps not strange, simply a preordained pattern foreshadowing the final disclosure. Though what that could be, she'd no idea. Reggie had never confided in her, but the secret he'd shared with William and Laurence had, in the end, overshadowed his death. And she knew it was rooted in that third expedition.

She rested her head against the pillows, closing her eyes and letting the memories come, as she attempted yet again to uncover those roots.

At the time, William Langley's illness had been uppermost in their minds, and the edginess she detected in both Reggie and Laurence was explained by that. Even so, since he was over the worst by the time they reached home, their constant trips to Broadminster had struck her as excessive. Then had come the bombshell, the suggestion that they leave their comfortable home in Oxted and move to Broadshire themselves.

She stirred, and the delicate teacup, still beneath her fingers, rattled on its saucer. Gently she pushed the wheeled trolley further down the bed. She had hinted to Janis that Isabelle's health was a deciding factor in the move; in truth, Isabelle had been as reluctant as herself to be uprooted. But for some reason she'd never understood, both Reggie and Laurence were determined to move closer to William. Her objections to leaving friends, voluntary work, her beloved garden, all had been overridden with uncharacteristic impatience. As Rowena was at boarding school, her education wouldn't be affected. There was nothing, she was told, to keep them in Surrey.

During those months of upheaval, Reggie had been like a stranger, nervous and irritable, and with occasional outbursts of a febrile excitement that alarmed her. Only after they were installed here at Cajabamba—and how she'd argued against that ridiculous name—had he begun to relax, though the visits to William were as regular as ever.

A tap on the door disturbed her musings, and Edith came in to remove the tray.

"Have Mrs. Coverdale and the children left yet?"

"No, my lady. Mr. Miles is coming for them at ten."

"I hope the road conditions aren't too bad. It seems madness to make unnecessary journeys in this weather, but when you're young, such things don't worry you."

"No, my lady," said Edith dutifully, closing the door behind her. Thoughtfully, Lady Peel reached for her bedside telephone.

Miles had hardly spoken since they set out and Jan, in the front seat beside him, wondered if he were regretting his invitation. Even the children sat in silence, watching the snowy landscape; but they'd been quiet ever since Lily's death, and her repeated assurances had failed to comfort them. That much was apparent from Julie's frightened question last night. She really must have a talk with them, and set their minds at rest. If only Roger were here, to advise her what to say.

Shying from thoughts of Roger, she concentrated on the present. At least the main road was clear, but on either side of it the snow, piled into high banks, dwarfed them with its whiteness, seeming to threaten an icy oblivion. She wondered what extremes of temperature Edward and Rowena would be facing.

And at the thought of Peru, her mind switched back to the book, with its story of Inca treasure and the pencilled exclamation mark. Who had drawn it? When, and why? Was it merely a reader's impatience with what he saw as exaggerated claims—

emeralds as large as quails' eggs? Or had those marks some deeper meaning?

Miles spoke suddenly, making her jump. "Have you ever been to Ringmere?"

"Once, as a child. But that was in summer."

"Then you wouldn't have seen the Bewick's swans."

Jan turned to smile at him. "You sound very knowledgeable!"

"I've always been interested in birds. It's amazing what they've achieved at these places; by ringing the birds, they've discovered that the same ones return year after year, and there are special breeding facilities for threatened species."

"Will there be penguins?" Ben asked from the back seat.

Miles laughed. "Afraid not. It might look like the North Pole out there, but we can't rise to penguins." He added more seriously, "It's not a zoo, Ben. These are mainly wild birds, who come here by choice from all over the world."

"From Australia?"

"Yes, there are even black swans from Australia."

"Are we nearly there?" Julie asked hopefully.

"Ten more minutes." Miles turned off the road at a signpost. "You'd better wrap up warmly, it'll be bitter out there."

"So why the hell was his name in the diary?" The Detective Superintendant's bright eyes bored into Webb's, and he shifted his weight on the narrow chair.

"Because he met Sinclair, who Marriott was watching. It was clear from the notebooks that he'd been monitoring Sinclair's lunch engagements for some time. Half a dozen or so are listed, all at the Commodore, with the name of the other party noted and the duration of the meeting."

"And what do you think was behind it?"

"Well, sir, since the notes were for Marriott's own use, they aren't too explicit."

"But reading between the lines?" queried Fleming, his head on one side.

"I'd say the lunches had a rather special line in 'afters.' "

"Ha! Go on."

"In each case, they were joined by the same young lady at the coffee stage. At least, that's what the timing of her arrival seems to indicate."

"And how long did she stay?"

"Between one and two hours."

"Very cosy. Then they all left separately?"

"Oh yes. Sinclair usually emerged about two-thirty and the other two an hour or so later, with a ten-minute interval between them."

"Any names we might know?"

"Mainly bankers and investment advisers."

"Sinclair might well have topped Marriott, if he discovered he was on to him. As to his other activities, no doubt they'll be of interest to Wood Street. Right, Spider, look into him, will you. Managing all right without Bates?"

"I wouldn't refuse a replacement, sir."

"See what I can do."

The family Rover had been sold during Sir Reginald's last illness, and ever since, Lady Peel, who disliked driving, had hired a car whenever she required transport. She always used the same firm, and having expressed a preference for a particular driver, the firm ensured whenever possible that he was available. Fred Perkins jokingly described himself as "Her Ladyship's chauffeur." He had taken the trouble to note the old lady's whims; the speed at which she liked to travel, that she required a rug over her knees, that she was not averse to small talk unless she indicated otherwise. Today, the old girl had something on her mind, and by the tone in which she returned his greeting, Fred knew this would be a silent ride. Going to see her solicitor, too.

He turned off Broad Street into Monks' Walk. On their right, the Minster Green was green no longer, but lay like a frozen moonscape beneath the snow. With the imposing cathedral soaring behind, the scene resembled a Christmas card. Snow before Christmas was all very well, but once it was over, Fred couldn't be doing with it. Furthermore, despite the fact that

Twelfth Night had passed, tired-looking Christmas trees still protruded from wrought-iron balconies above the shop fronts, while on the pavement below hardy shoppers searched for bargains in the sales.

He turned left into George Street and drew up outside the offices of Bradshaw and Campbell. They were on the first floor, but he knew one of the clerks would be on the look-out for his charge, to escort her up the linoleumed stairs.

"Wait for me, Perkins," instructed Her Ladyship, with sublime disregard for the yellow lines on each side of the road. Fred touched his cap. He'd park in the yard of the coffee-house opposite—Jack Lindsay was a pal of his. A seat at a window table would enable him to keep a look-out and at the same time warm himself with a cup of coffee. There were worse jobs on such a morning.

"Good morning, Mr. Bradshaw."

Leonard Hargreaves, senior partner of the firm, bowed over the extended hand with old-fashioned courtesy. He had explained at their first meeting that both Mr. Bradshaw and Mr. Campbell were long since departed, but if his valued client wished to address him thus, he would not complain. A cup of fresh coffee was produced, and some shortbread fingers.

"Now, Lady Peel, how can we be of service?"

The old lady hesitated. "I hope what I'm about to ask won't infringe any professional ethics, Mr. Bradshaw. What I wish to know is whether my late husband left any instructions to be carried out after his death."

"No, my lady."

She fixed him with her pale blue eyes. "He didn't, or you're not free to answer my question?"

"We held nothing for action after Sir Reginald's death. Other than his will, of course." Mr. Hargreaves hesitated. "Now that I think of it, he did lodge a letter with us some years ago, but he later reclaimed it."

"Ah!" The old lady's back straightened. "When was it deposited?"

"When Sir Reginald first engaged us to act for him, on his arrival in Broadminster."

"In nineteen fifty-six?"

"It would be about then, yes."

"And what were his instructions?"

"That it was to be delivered three calendar months after the death of the last survivor of himself, Mr. Laurence Coady and Mr. William Langley."

Lady Peel gazed at him expectantly. "To be delivered to me?"

"Er—no, my lady. To your daughter, Miss Rowena Peel as she then was."

That had been a shock, he could see. Uncomfortably, Mr. Hargreaves wondered, too late, if the information should have been withheld.

"And you say he reclaimed it," she said after a moment. "When was that?"

"After the death of Mr. Langley, ten years ago."

"Did my husband infer he was going to destroy the letter, or hand it to my daughter himself?"

"He merely requested its return, my lady."

She paused, then asked diffidently, "Did you by any chance also act for William Langley and Laurence Coady?"

"No, my lady."

And if he had, it would have been no help. Answering an innocuous question about her own husband was one thing; inquiries about other clients would have been respectfully fielded.

"Very well, Mr. Bradshaw, thank you. I shan't take up any more of your time."

As she accepted the arm of the clerk to assist her downstairs, Lady Peel found her curiosity whetted rather than satisfied by her visit. The date that Reggie had deposited the letter suggested it was the result of a joint decision. No doubt Laurence and William had written similar ones. Had they, too, later reclaimed them? If not, Edward, Janis and Miles were due to receive them any day—three calendar months after Reggie's death.

But *why*, she asked herself, as Perkins helped her into the car and arranged the rug over her knees, had Reggie changed his mind? And had he destroyed the letter, or given it to Rowena? She felt certain that whether or not Rowena had received it, that letter would have held the answer to the unexplained mystery of that last shared expedition.

Tony Rollo's breakfast deliberations also resulted in a phone call, though it was mid-morning before he'd the chance to make it. When his secretary finally left him, a sheaf of correspondence in her hands, he pulled the instrument towards him and re-quested an outside line.

"Roy?" he said urgently. "It's Tony Rollo."

"My dear chap! How's the world treating you?"

Not for the first time, the bluff friendliness struck Rollo as false. "Diabolically," he answered shortly. "The police have been here."

"Police?" Sinclair's voice sharpened. "What the hell for?"

"Asking questions about this man that was murdered. Marri-ott. I presume you knew him?"

"The journalist, you mean? I knew he was sniffing round, but he'd nothing to go on. How the hell did they connect him with you?"

"God knows, but they thought it was him I'd lunched with in November."

"I sincerely hope you didn't enlighten them?" The silken tones were no longer friendly.

"Be reasonable, Roy; I had to. They already knew I was there —the time we arrived, the time we left."

"Sweet mercy," said Sinclair softly. "And Camilla?"

"She wasn't mentioned, but I should think they know about her."

"And they got all this from that bloody journalist?"

"Must have done."

"I'd give a lot to know what else they dug up."

"You'll soon find out," Rollo said ironically. "They'll be up to see you, you can bet. I'm just warning you, so you can cover your tracks. For all our sakes." He replaced the receiver and wiped a hand wearily over his face. Then, with a sigh, he returned to the morning's business.

It was blissfully warm in the Research and Education Centre, but outside the plate-glass windows, sleet fell horizontally over the bleak stretches of water. A group of visitors, muffled against the cold, were throwing crusts to a jostling crowd of birds, some of which had come out of the water and were waddling among their benefactors' legs. A little girl, nervous of their proximity, began to cry, her voice a thin wail through the thick glass.

Jan left the children watching the scene outside, and went over to the wall maps showing the natural habitat of the birds. Instinctively, she paused at the one of South America.

"Thinking of your dear brother?" Miles inquired, handing her a plastic cup of coffee.

"Just Peru generally. Sorry, I know it bores you."

"I'm surprised it doesn't bore you, too. We're in the same position, after all." He sipped his coffee, his eyes on the map. "Have you ever wondered," he said unexpectedly, "why neither of our fathers went back after fifty-five?"

Jan turned to him in surprise. "Yes, I have. What's more, the police were asking, too."

Miles frowned. "What the hell's it got to do with them?"

"I don't know. Miles, can I tell you something rather odd? I was reading a book of Sir Reginald's last night, and—"

"Come *on*, Mum!" Ben had appeared at her side and was tugging impatiently at her hand. "It's stopped snowing—let's go out and look at the geese."

With a glance of smiling apology at Miles, Jan allowed herself to be led towards the door. After a moment, abandoning his coffee on a convenient shelf, Miles followed them.

"The trouble is," Webb said heavily, as they reached the outskirts of Broadminster, "there are two possible motives for Marriott's death. Either he was treading on someone's toes, or he was killed to implicate Edward Langley. He *might* have died simply because he looked like Langley, though the killer must have known he wasn't. If he was close enough to steal Langley's wallet, he probably knows him personally."

"We don't know it was the killer who stole the wallet," Jackson objected, negotiating a right-hand turn. "Marriott might have been on to something about Langley, and took his wallet to try to verify it. Langley could have caught him at it, and given chase."

"And killed him, you mean? Then why and by whom was Lily Carr murdered?"

"Perhaps we'll find out now," Jackson commented, drawing up outside a small chalet bungalow. No one had troubled to clear the path, and the detectives crunched over the snow to the front door. It was opened at their knock by a pale, red-eyed young woman who had a child clinging to her skirt.

Webb introduced himself, and she stepped to one side. In the hall they were met by a strong smell of damp washing, the cause of which was apparent as they were shown into the back room. A clothes-horse stood in front of the fire, festooned with nappies. A baby of some six months lay kicking in a play-pen and the floor was littered with toys. The woman pushed her lank hair off her face.

"Sit down, if you can find a place."

Jackson, the father, paused for a look at the kicking baby, and was rewarded by a toothless grin. Webb removed a legless teddy bear from a shabby wicker chair and seated himself.

"I'm sorry to trouble you at such a time, Mrs. Bennett, but I'm sure you'll appreciate it's necessary. You lived with your mother?" he added somewhat unnecessarily.

The woman's eyes filled. "That's right. She took me and the kids in when Pete went off."

"And when was that?"

"Soon after the baby was born. Said he was fed up with flipping kids. How did he think I felt?"

"Did your husband ever knock you about?"

She looked at him in surprise. "Sometimes, when he'd been

to the pub. He was always sorry after—and he never laid a finger on the kids. That I will say for him."

"Did he get on well with your mother?"

The direction of the questioning finally reached her, and she hurried to defend her erring husband. "He wouldn't knock her over the head, if that's what you're getting at. If he *had* wanted to, he'd have done it here, wouldn't he, not up at Rylands?" She paused. "Anyway," she added defiantly, "he'd a lot of time for Mum, had Pete—the way she'd brought me up after Dad was killed, and all."

"Is there anyone you can think of who might have wished your mother harm?"

She moved impatiently. "Of course not. Why should they? Mum wouldn't have hurt a fly." Her mouth trembled. "Look— it's obvious, isn't it? A burglar broke in expecting the house to be empty, and found Mum there. She wouldn't have stood a chance." She began to weep softly.

She was probably right, at that, Jackson reflected, pen poised over his notebook. This was a necessary but unrewarding task and he'd be glad when it was over. Other people's grief distressed him, made him feel like a voyeur. Same on the telly, nowadays. Every time you switched on, some poor blighter was being asked how they felt on hearing that their husband or mother or son had been killed.

Methodically he noted down the governor's questions and the woman's replies. Could do with a cuppa, but it didn't look likely. The interview ground on, with the soft gurgling of the baby in the background and the rhythmic squeak of a rocking horse as the little girl rode endlessly backwards and forwards.

Hard on the kids to be deserted twice, even if the second time wasn't deliberate. Lost their Dad and lost their Gran, poor little perishers, and it was anyone's guess how long the mother'd be able to cope.

With a sense of relief he saw Webb getting to his feet. They were free to go.

"Not much joy there," he offered, as they crunched their way back to the car.

"In more ways than one," grunted Webb. "We'll call in at Court Lane and see how the house-to-house is going. And," he added, with a sidelong glance at Jackson, "no doubt we'll be offered a cup of tea."

Going home through the snow-lit country darkness, the children chatted softly in the back seat about the strange and beautiful creatures they'd seen. Jan, relaxed now in the warm car after the stimulating cold outside, was aware of their voices only as undulating waves of sound. It had been a happy day, a welcome respite from the worries and fears that awaited her return, and she was grateful to Miles for arranging it.

The visit to his mews house offered an extended moratorium, and while she moved, entranced, from one oil painting to another, read the spines of the volumes in the bookcase, and studied the marble bust on its plinth, the children ran up the stairs and hung over the balcony rail. They were equally enthralled by the hidden, pocket-sized kitchen and the carved animals on the low tables.

"I hope you're well insured!" Jan commented. "All this must be worth a fortune."

"I buy only what I like," Miles replied, handing her a glass of wine. "A friend of mine, Richard Mowbray, owns an antique shop in Monks' Walk, and lets me know when anything interesting comes in."

"Not Pennyfarthings?"

"That's the one. Have you been in?"

"I bought Edward and Rowena's Christmas presents there. They said something about a murder," she added with assumed nonchalance.

"There've been murders in many places, Jan. If you let that worry you, you'd never go back to Rylands."

She shuddered and sipped her wine. He was right. It had startled her, at Christmas, to learn of the Pennyfarthings murder. She'd little thought that two more would touch her much more closely.

To escape the thought, she moved over to the desk, whose surface was covered with sketches and artwork.

"Is this the project you were telling me about?"

He joined her. "That's right. Three hundred years of Buckhurst Grange and the Cleverleys. The family crest, here, will feature on second-class stamps, and this miniaturised photo of the house on first-class. For higher denominations, I've looked out portraits of outstanding members of the family, starting with the first Lord Cleverley."

"It all looks most impressive."

"I'm doing the TV tie-in at the moment. It's going quite well, but we're at a delicate stage of negotiations and I'll breathe more freely once it all receives committee approval. Now"—he walked back to the fire and threw on another log—"I've put plates to warm in the oven. Who'll come with me to the Chinese to choose our supper?"

"I will!" said both children together.

"Then if you'll tell me where things are, I'll lay the table," Jan offered.

It was an informal and enjoyable meal, with Miles more relaxed than she'd seen him. Again it surprised her that, unused to children as he was, he should be so natural with them.

Later, as she was washing the dishes at the sink in the cupboard, he commented, "You mentioned a book of Sir Reginald's."

"Oh, yes." Jan glanced over her shoulder. The children were just behind her, playing with a beautiful old Solitaire set. "It wasn't important," she said. She did not wish to speak about jewels in their hearing till she'd discovered what was worrying them.

"But you've aroused my curiosity."

"Another time," she answered quietly.

"Ah, I see. *Pas devant les enfants.* Very well, I'll contain myself." He dried a glass carefully and reached above her to place it on a shelf, and his sudden closeness sent an uncontrollable *frisson* through her body which she prayed he hadn't noticed. Hastily she tipped the water away, dried her hands, and moved out of the enforced intimacy of the tiny kitchen.

But half an hour later, when the children ran ahead of her into the hall of Cajabamba and she turned to Miles for a last word of thanks, it was clear her reaction had been noted. With a swiftness that took her by surprise, he bent forward and kissed her, briefly but penetratingly. Then he turned and ran back down the steps, leaving her weak and shaking, leaning against the door-frame for support. With an effort she straightened and closed the door, on Miles, and she hoped, on the incident. But her trembling body, deprived for months now of its lovemaking, warned her that in future she must be careful not to be alone with Miles.

CHAPTER 10

Saturday morning, and still the snow fell. Jan stood at the window watching the soft, uneven flakes landing on the sill, restlessly wondering how they should pass the day. With half her mind, she wanted to return to Rylands; despite the horror, it was more home than the elderly ambience of Cajabamba. And they couldn't stay here for the three and a half weeks that remained of their visit; it would be an imposition on Lady Peel and too restricting for the children.

Yet the other half of her shrank from the thought of being alone, surrounded by the silent snow, looking fearfully for unauthorized footsteps round the house.

She turned back into the room. Lady Peel had not yet come down, and the children were colouring some books they'd bought at Ringmere. At least she could have the talk with them that she'd been promising herself. She walked over to the games table and sat down opposite Julie.

"I have some questions I'd like to ask you both," she said quietly. "First, Ben, why did you tell Julie the man who killed Lily would kill you, too? And Julie, what did you mean by saying the Crown Jewels weren't as good as Aunt Rowena's?"

The children had both looked up, and a warning glance passed between them.

"I want the truth," Jan continued. "You've both been worried about something, and I want to know what it is."

There was a long silence, then Ben said gruffly, "OK, we'll tell you if you'll promise not to be cross."

"Well?"

He wriggled on his chair, looking quickly at his sister and then away again. "Remember the morning we explored the house, and then went to play upstairs?"

"I remember."

"Well, there was nothing interesting in the attics, so Julie decided to dress up. She was going to put on your cocktail frock, but then Lotus hooked open Aunt Rowena's door. Lily couldn't have closed it properly when she'd been dusting."

"Go on."

Ben flushed and started doodling on his crayoning book. "Well, you know what a fuss she'd made, when I nearly went in by mistake. We thought since the door was open, we'd have a look and see what was so marvellous. It seemed pretty ordinary, but there was a belt hanging out of the wardrobe and Lotus started playing with it. We thought she'd scratch the leather, so we opened the door to push it inside. And when Julie saw Aunt Rowena's clothes, she thought it would be more fun to dress up in them."

Jan opened her mouth to remonstrate, and closed it again. Julie let the whine creep into her voice. "We knew you'd be cross, so we didn't want to tell you."

"Go on," Jan said again.

It was Julie who continued. "Well, I tried on a pair of high-heels, but when I tried to walk in them, I wobbled so much I nearly fell, and I—I put out a hand to steady myself."

"Yes?" Somehow, this must be important, at least to the children.

"But the clothes on the rail just swung back and I lost my balance and fell through them, banging against the back of the wardrobe. And—and it started to open."

Jan stared at her. "To *open?* What on earth—"

"Like a secret passage," said Ben. "The back of the wardrobe started to slide back, and because Julie was leaning against it, she half fell inside."

"But inside what? You're not trying to tell me there's a secret passage at Rylands?"

But they didn't smile with her. "Not a passage," Ben said seriously, "but there was a tiny room behind there."

"And that's where the jewels were, round someone's neck," Julie said in a rush.

Jan's mouth went dry. "Will you explain that?"

"I thought at first it was a real person, like in my dream, and I was very scared, but it was only a dummy after all."

Jan said slowly, "Look, darling, you must be mistaken. You're talking about a dark space behind a wardrobe. You *couldn't* have seen anything clearly. You must just have *thought* you—"

"It wasn't dark," Ben interrupted. "A light came on in the wardrobe when we opened the door. It was shining straight onto the jewels, and a round gold thing."

Jan said faintly, "So what did you do?"

"Well, nothing. Everything happened so quickly. One minute we were staring in, then Julie stood up and took her hand off the wood, and the back slid shut again."

Julie shuddered. "I was nearly shut inside." That, too, had figured in her nightmare.

Ben said, "So when the burglar came, we knew what he was looking for. And I thought if he found out we'd seen the jewels, he'd come after us. So we decided not to say anything."

"You never went back for another look?"

Again the exchanged glance. "We did try," Julie confessed with bent head. "But though we pressed and pressed, it wouldn't open."

"When you say wardrobe, you mean it was a fitted one, not free-standing as they are here?"

"It was built in, like we have at home."

"But it just doesn't make sense. The house isn't old enough for secret rooms."

"It wasn't really a room," Ben said consideringly, "more like a cupboard. We wondered if Grandpa'd used it, when it was his and Granny's room."

Counter-intelligence. Her father'd been in counter-intelligence. Had he by any chance had the space made during the War, to hide a radio set, secret documents? As to the jewels, perhaps Rowena used it as an enlarged safe. It would explain why she hadn't wanted the children in her room.

She said, "Can you describe exactly what you saw?"

Ben thought for a moment while Julie silently went on with her crayoning. "They were on a little table, the gold thing in front, and behind it a lady's head and shoulders like they have in shop windows, with the jewels draped round it, shining brightly in the light."

"So it was a necklace you saw?"

"I suppose so."

"And that was all? No rings or bangles?"

"We didn't see anything else."

"Well, it was lucky it was well hidden, and the burglar didn't find it." Though how could he have known about it?

There was a tap on the door and Edith came in with coffee and the children's milk. "Her Ladyship will be down in a minute," she reported.

Jan stood up, glad of the interruption. The overdue discussion was behind her, and the children's minds set at rest. But her own still circled round the necklace, beautiful and unseen in its hiding place. Why was it so elaborately displayed, instead of being safely in its box? And what was the "round gold thing" Ben had mentioned? A tray of some sort? Most puzzling of all, had the children really seen what they said, or was it part of some complicated make-believe that they'd come to accept as the truth? All in all, that seemed the most likely explanation.

"David? I hope I'm not interrupting anything?"

"Hello, Hannah." Surprise sounded in his voice. She very seldom rang him at the station. "What can I do for you?"

"I tried to phone last night, but there was no reply. Could you possibly call round? I've learned something which might interest you—to do with the case."

He smiled. "That's a tempting prospect, mixing business with pleasure."

"And if you could stretch it to include lunch—"

"Best offer I've had all week." His eyes went to the wall clock. "One o'clock suit you?"

"Fine. See you then."

She was wearing a pale blue jumper and fawn slacks, and she looked delectable. Webb, who maintained that no woman over thirty should wear trousers, happily acknowledged she was an exception. A spicy smell was emanating from the kitchen, and he found he was hungrier than he'd realized; and, as he sat down in his usual chair, more tired. It was very tempting to relax, to imagine this was an ordinary Saturday afternoon and his time was his own.

"Drink?" Hannah inquired from the doorway.

"I'd better stick to beer, love, if you've got some."

"Of course I have."

He watched her as she came towards him, imprinting another picture of her on his memory: thick, tawny hair, today held back with a tortoise-shell band; wide forehead, clear grey eyes. Better stop the inventory before his feelings got the better of him. He took the glass from her.

"Know how I'd like to spend the afternoon?"

She laughed. "From the look in your eyes, I can guess."

"Why can't murder cases finish neatly on Friday evenings?"

"You tell me."

They had an unspoken rule not to discuss their work over meals. Today, however, knowing his time was limited, Hannah waived it.

"Remember asking me about Laurence Coady?" she said, as she ladled a fragrant curry onto his plate.

"I do."

"Well, in yesterday's Current Affairs class they were discussing the present expedition, and one of the girls said Coady came to give a talk to the school when her mother was head girl."

"Really? When would that have been?"

"July, nineteen-sixty. What's more, the talk was written up in the school magazine, and Karen's mother still has a copy. I haven't seen it myself, but apparently he told them he'd written a book."

"*Coady* had? Have you ever heard of it?"

"No—I got the impression it's never been published. It was about the third expedition he went on with Langley and Peel."

Webb laid down his fork. "Was it, indeed? That could be interesting. Where does this family live?"

"Lethbridge Close, up by the golf club."

"Right, if I can use your phone, I'll see if they're home this afternoon."

Lethbridge Close was a small cul-de-sac off the Lethbridge Road. Mrs. Stevens was watching for him, and opened the door as his car pulled up outside.

"Chief Inspector Webb? Do come in."

She was a small woman in her mid-forties, her face saved from plainness by magnificent brown eyes. She was wearing a red kilt in some obscure tartan—though most tartans were obscure to Webb—and a cashmere sweater with a scarf at her throat.

"If you'd like to come through, I have the magazine ready for you. And perhaps you'd care for some coffee?"

The house was modern and spacious, with patio doors giving onto a snow-covered garden. A tall, thin man stood up as they entered, whom Mrs. Stevens introduced as her husband. Their daughter was not present.

Webb seated himself on a comfortable sofa and picked up the magazine. On the front cover were the words "Ashbourne School for Girls," and beneath them the school shield which he'd seen before, with the motto curved round the top of it. Along the foot of the page were the words "Summer 1960."

"It's on page nineteen," Mrs. Stevens said, smoothing her kilt as she sat down by the coffee-pot.

Webb accepted a cup from her husband and settled back to read.

"One of the outstanding events of the term was a visit by the explorer, Mr. Laurence Coady, who gave us an illustrated talk on Peru. He had many stories to tell about the Incas and their fabulous wealth, which was destroyed by the *conquistadores.* There was a garden in Cuzco where everything was made of gold, beautifully worked flowers and leaves, and replicas of maize with silver stems and golden ears.

"Mr. Coady also told us some Inca legends, about the Sun

God who sent his children to teach the natives civilization, and of white-bearded men coming out of Lake Titicaca, and it was very exciting to see on the screen the places he was talking about.

"At the end of the talk he agreed to answer questions. Alice Manning asked about the Nazca lines in the desert, and Pippa Clyde wanted to know more about the Amazon. Then Janet Forsyth asked Mr. Coady when he'd be going back to Peru. To our surprise, he said he was never going back. Janet asked him why, and he said the answer was in a book he'd written about the last expedition. However, it wouldn't be published till after his death and that of his fellow explorers, because it contained highly sensitive material.

"Miss Seymour proposed a vote of thanks, and everyone expressed their enjoyment of the talk with prolonged applause."

Webb looked up and met Mrs. Stevens' eye. "I believe you were actually at the talk, ma'am?"

"Yes, I was."

"Does your recollection agree with this account?"

"I think so, yes."

"And what was your impression of Laurence Coady?"

"He was rather a romantic figure, we thought—tall, dark and brooding." It could, Webb thought, be a description of his son. "Then, of course, he disappeared from public view and became something of a recluse. I think that talk was one of the last he gave."

"Perhaps he wasn't prepared to be questioned any more on the third expedition."

"Do you know, you could be right. I never thought of that." She hesitated. "Didn't I read recently of the death of Sir Reginald Peel? Perhaps Mr. Coady's book will be published at last."

"If he really did write one. He could have been simply fobbing off questions and creating a mystery." But Webb didn't believe that. In nineteen-sixty, he was sure, the manuscript had existed. The question was, did it now?

Webb rose to his feet. "I'm extremely grateful to you for

allowing me to read this. Would you mind if I took it with me? It'll be returned as soon as we've finished with it."

"By all means, if you think it will help." She hesitated. "Karen thought it was something to do with that body that was found at Chedbury?"

"It could very well be. Thank you for your help, Mrs. Stevens —and the coffee."

Jackson was waiting in the office when he got back to Carrington Street. "Guess where we're going?" Webb greeted him.

Jackson grinned. "Peru?"

"You could well be right."

"You're not serious, guv?"

"Oh, but I am. The further this case progresses, the more urgent it becomes to interview Langley. We thought from the beginning the answer lay at least partly with him. It's time we learned how much of it. Still, we're not setting off straight away. Broadminster will do for this afternoon."

"Who are we going to see this time?"

"In the absence of the Langleys, Miles Coady and Janis Coverdale. The descendants of the original explorers."

In the car, Webb told Jackson about the school magazine.

"Well, we might have guessed, mightn't we? They all do it, these blokes."

"Do what?"

"Write books. As soon as they set foot back in dear old Blighty, they whip out the old ballpoint and write their memoirs."

"But they usually send them hot-foot to the publishers. They don't sit on them till they've no hope of earning any royalties."

"What do you reckon he meant by 'highly sensitive material'?"

"God knows. Could be libellous, I suppose."

Jackson chuckled. "Then he was wise to get out of the way first. Still, if it was, no publisher would touch it, would they?"

Webb shrugged. "It will be interesting to hear what Master Miles has to say."

Coady greeted them with a blank face. They received the impression that they were an unwelcome interruption to his schedule. "Yes, Chief Inspector? What is it this time? I've already given an account of my movements on Wednesday, though as no doubt you know, innocent people seldom have alibis."

"This is a different matter, sir." Webb's tone was mild, but he was watching the man closely. "Could you tell us if your father ever wrote a book?"

"A book?" Coady repeated, and Webb could have sworn it was to gain time.

"That's right, sir. About the expedition in fifty-five."

"It's a bit late to start asking, isn't it? It would have come out thirty-odd years ago."

"Not," Webb said calmly, "if he arranged for it to be published after his death. And," he continued over Coady's interruption, "that of his fellow explorers."

Coady stared at him. "What's suddenly brought this up?"

"A school magazine. Your father gave a talk in nineteen-sixty in which he stated that he'd written a book about his last expedition. We wondered if you knew anything about it."

"Nothing whatever." The man's eyes held his, and Webb sensed a battle of wills. He was also sure Coady was lying. But he allowed his eyes to drop first.

"Very well, sir. Perhaps Mrs. Coverdale can help us."

"If I can't, I don't see how she can."

"It's worth a try. Sorry to have troubled you."

They came out of the mews and stood on Clarence Way, turning up their collars as the cold north wind buffeted them. "We'll leave the car where it is and walk," Webb said. "Which, come to think of it, is what Marriott did. Question is, where did he walk to?"

"You mean somewhere like this, where there's no parking?"

"A tempting thought. I don't trust Coady, but I'm damned if I see what connection he had with Marriott. And don't forget the Bank was within walking distance of the car park, too. Anyway, we'll call in at Cavendish Road and see how the lab boys are doing."

At Rylands, they found the forensic team completing their examination. "No reason why the family can't move back," the senior man told Webb. "We've got all the samples we can find, and you'll have the results within a couple of days."

At the Peel household, both Janis Coverdale and Lady Peel denied knowledge of a book, though the old lady seemed shaken by the question.

"A book!" she repeated, but it was a statement rather than a query, as though it offered a solution to some puzzle. "Why do you ask?" she added after a moment, and Webb again explained about the magazine.

"How extraordinary. I never thought of a book. And his son knows nothing about it?"

"He says not."

She looked up at him. "If it came to light, would the families have a chance to read it before publication?"

"It could be arranged, but there's no one left to confirm or deny the contents." He paused. "Lady Peel, were you expecting something to come to light after your husband's death?"

She met his eyes. "Yes, Chief Inspector, I believe I was."

"Could you tell me why?"

She was silent for a moment, looking down at her clasped hands. Then she said quietly, "Until nineteen fifty-five, my husband had no secrets from me. He was not a secretive man."

"And after that?"

"After that, there was something. I'd hoped he might have left me a letter, to explain—apologize."

"And he didn't?"

"No." Lady Peel straightened her back. "I may as well tell you —in any case you'd find out—that I went to see my solicitor yesterday, specifically to ask that question. And he told me a curious thing. When we first came here from Surrey, my husband did indeed deposit a letter with him, but it was addressed to my daughter, not myself. It was to be delivered three calendar months after the last of them had died. As it happened, Reginald himself."

"So it's awaiting her return from Peru?"

"No. My husband withdrew it, ten years ago." She glanced across at Jan. "After the death of Mr. William Langley."

"And did he give it to your daughter?"

"I don't know. It was never mentioned in my hearing."

"So you've no idea what it contained?"

"None whatsoever."

"What about you, Mrs. Coverdale? Have you received any notification from your father's solicitors?"

She shook her head, her wide eyes on his face, and Webb turned back to the older woman. "Did your solicitor act for the others, by any chance?"

Lady Peel smiled. "No, I ascertained that much, after which my hands were tied; but yours won't be. Chief Inspector, do you think this is connected with the murders?"

"Yes, Lady Peel, I do. In fact, I intend to fly out to Peru next week, to see Mr. and Mrs. Langley. If you can advise me the best way of contacting them, I'd be very grateful."

The old lady paled, and Jan broke in, "But you don't think *they've* anything to do with it?"

"As I explained before, Mrs. Coverdale, your half-brother is certainly implicated, though whether voluntarily or not I can't say." He paused. "Don't forget he was still in the country at the time of the first death. Do you know where they are at the moment?"

Jan swallowed. "Not accurately. Somewhere between Cuzco and Cajabamba."

"Well, no doubt once we get out there, we can contact them by radio."

She shook her head. "Radios are useless in the jungle. VHF only works for about five miles, and high frequency sets are too heavy. They need a charging engine and an experienced operator, and Edward says they're not worth the trouble. But he'll have left a rear party in Cuzco. They'll be able to help you."

He was about to rise, but she put out a hand to detain him.

"Chief Inspector, there's something else I've been meaning to tell you. My mother-in-law phoned on Thursday. She'd tried to ring me the day before, when we were in London."

Webb stiffened. "Yes?"

"Mrs. Carr answered the phone."

"What time was this, Mrs. Coverdale?"

"About lunch-time, she said. She couldn't be more definite." Jan paused. "Is it any help?"

"It's useful confirmation. We've established lunch-time as the most likely time of death. A few minutes either way will only make a difference if someone has an alibi." He stood up, nodding to Jackson. "Thank you for passing on the information. I'll be in touch again before we leave for Peru. In the meantime, the lab has finished at the other house. You and the children are free to go back."

After the policemen had gone, Jan brought *Treasures of the Incas* down from her bedroom, and showed the pencil mark to Lady Peel.

"Have you any idea what that means?" she asked.

The old lady read through the page. "I can't imagine, dear."

"Did Sir Reginald ever mention these particular jewels?"

"Not that I remember. He'd hoped to find some treasure at Cajabamba, though he knew it was unlikely. As he told me, the Incas had been so sure of their supremacy and the honesty of their subjects that they didn't worry about security. Consequently when their empire fell, everything was there to be taken."

"Not quite everything, it seems," Jan answered thoughtfully.

It was eight o'clock when Webb let himself into his flat, grateful for its welcoming warmth. God bless central heating, especially after a day in the January cold.

And thank God, also, for fish and chips. Usually, he enjoyed preparing his meal, but this evening he was impatient to get down to some sketching.

Having deposited his supper in the oven, he went to the

living-room, pausing at the window as he always did to look
down the hill to the town nestling at its foot, its thoroughfares
easily identified by orange lamps strung in the darkness.

It was a ritual now, a conscious relaxation, to distance himself
visually as well as mentally from his working life. Tonight, the
sodium lights turned the snow beneath them to gold, and it
looked like some strange desertland out there. There was desert
in Peru, as well as jungle and mountains.

So much for the shedding of work, he told himself ruefully.
The thought of the coming trip exhilarated him, though he was
also apprehensive. For the first time he wouldn't be operating
on home ground, and the advantage of knowing the territory
would belong not to him but to Edward Langley. As a detective,
he knew the importance of this.

He needed therefore to clarify his thoughts by setting them
on paper, hoping that this visual method, as so often in the past,
would lead him in a new direction. To begin with Marriott, an
investigative journalist makes enemies, but whose secret was
important enough to kill for? Find the motive, and you find the
murderer. Sometimes.

He drew the curtains and poured himself a drink, aware of the
growing need for pencil and paper. This usually came later in a
case—they were only six days into this one—but there were so
many disparate threads that he needed to draw them into a
composite picture.

He ate quickly and without enjoyment, a mere stoking up of
energy for the task ahead. As soon as he finished, he removed
the tray and set up his easel, his mind already slipping into
overdrive.

First, the *dramatis personae,* and here his skill as a cartoonist
helped, each figure instantly recognizable beneath his pencil. In
pride of place was the dead man, Guy Marriott, and circling him,
the owners of the wallets: Rollo, Cassidy, Coady and Langley.
Next, like artefacts buried with dead Pharaohs—and for all he
knew, dead Incas too—he drew the tools of their trades: a
cheque-book for Rollo, a calculator for the accountant Cassidy,

an easel for Coady, and for Langley, a long, narrow oblong representing Peru.

Then he stared broodingly down at them, tapping his pencil on his thumb-nail. Langley, they'd not so far questioned, but the other three denied knowing Marriott. Was one of them lying?

And how far was Sinclair involved? Was he also connected with Coady and Cassidy? The report from London should provide some answers. Thoughtfully, he sketched in associated locales: the hotel where the lunches were held, a building to denote the squash club, the Chedbury layby and its fallen tree. And following on that, those early inconsistencies—a shabby jacket with sequins on its lapel and a bandage which might or might not represent a mummy. Was there a hidden message there, and did it lead back more than thirty years?

Attempts to trace the clothes were proving difficult. He reckoned they were most likely bought in November, which was the date of the scraps of newspaper clinging to them, but so far inquiries at jumble sales throughout the county had proved negative.

He let the sheet drop to the floor, and selecting another, drew as faceless men those he'd never seen, the explorers whose long-past expedition overhung the case; and beside them, the women of the family—Lady Peel, Rowena Langley, and Janis Coverdale. Then he sketched an envelope, intended for posthumous delivery, but withdrawn from safekeeping. Had it been the only one? He'd checked with Coady who, like Mrs. Cloverdale, denied receiving a letter. And why had Sir Reginald withdrawn his? Because of Langley's death?

Webb studied the sketch of Lady Peel. She was an intelligent woman, capable of setting her mind to a mystery that intrigued her. Was it only now, after more than thirty years, that her curiosity was roused? How feasible was it that she'd uproot herself and move house, as Mrs. Coverdale had said, with no reasonable explanation?

Shaking his head, Webb progressed to the plainer features of Lily Carr. An avoidable death that one, due, surely, to unlucky chance. If she'd left the house with the Coverdales, she'd be alive today. And the only common factor between her death and that of Marriott was Edward Langley. His wallet, and his house.

The hours ticked away and Webb remained engrossed, training his concentration on one after another of the likenesses before him. The murderer was there, he felt sure. He was searching for some clue in the faces, some sign which his subconscious had noted but his conscious eye had missed. A weakness of character, an imbalance, which had led not to one murder, but two.

Perhaps, after all, he'd not enough to go on. He stood up, easing his aching back, and noted with surprise that it was past midnight. Still, the hours had not been wasted. They'd brought a more intimate understanding, a clearer awareness of virtues and weaknesses, and that could be the first step to unmasking the killer.

CHAPTER 11

The next morning, Jan and the children went back to Rylands, but not to stay; Lady Peel had been insistent on that.

"It's not safe, dear, till this nasty business is cleared up. And if, as the police think, the burglar didn't find what he was looking for, he's likely to try again, especially now the scientists have gone. Do please be sensible."

"But it's too much for you," Jan protested, "having the children rushing round all the time."

"Nonsense. They're perfectly well-behaved, and I'd be under considerably more strain worrying about you if you weren't here. I don't even like your going now, but I appreciate you need more things. Shall I ask Miles to go with you?"

"No, really, we'll be all right."

Jan hadn't seen Miles since his sudden kiss on Friday, and to her annoyance was apprehensive of their next meeting. She'd no wish to colour like a seventeen-year-old under his mocking gaze.

And there was another reason why she didn't want his company. She intended to examine Rowena's wardrobe, and find if there was any truth in the children's story.

The snow was at last melting, its crystal purity turned to sandy-coloured slush. Ben, boy-like, walked in the gutters, kicking the soft mounds ahead of him with his boots.

The clock on the tower of St. Benedict's chimed eleven as they turned into Cavendish Road. The last time they'd walked along here, Jan thought, was on their return from London, to find Lily dead. Could it really be only four days ago?

Julie's voice broke into her thoughts. "We should have brought Lotus with us. She'll be getting homesick."

"She's more settled at Cajabamba than we are," Jan replied. "Edith spoils her—she's quite happy."

"Lily spoiled her, too," said Julie with quivering lip, and Jan, contrite, took her hand.

The house seemed unaffected by its experience. Any mess the lab men had made had been tidied away, and apart from a faint smell, chemical in origin, it was as it had always been. But Jan knew she would not, ever again, look inside Edward's study.

They stood in a little group in the hall. Above them on the half-landing, the large, stained-glass window glowed softly in the winter sunshine.

Intercepting her thoughts, Ben said, "Shall we have a go at the wardrobe?" He had left his boots on the doormat, and stood in stockinged feet, one on top of the other.

"All right. Show me exactly what happened."

The entire ambience of the room had changed since her parents' day. A pale carpet in duck-egg blue replaced the old patterned one on which she had sat as a child. A chintz chair stood in the window, beside a low table bearing the ornaments about which Rowena had spoken: the cool greys and blues of Copenhagen porcelain, exquisite mounds of glass etched with the images of owls and otters.

The furniture, in fumed oak, had a silvery sheen and the old bed, in which she had opened her Christmas stockings, had given way to elegant twins, each with its cream-flowered duvet. Only the fitted wardrobe down the left-hand wall struck a chord in her memory, and it was this she had come to examine.

Julie ran across and pulled at the door, which folded back on itself to display a row of suits and dresses. As the children had said, a light came on automatically, illuminating the clothes.

With a feeling of guilt, Jan made a space between them, and her heart started thumping. Normally, a fitted wardrobe had as its back the wall against which it was built; here, a smooth sheet of wood met her eyes—surely an unnecessary refinement.

Watched breathlessly by the children, she stepped inside the cupboard and pressed her hands against the wood. Nothing happened. Working methodically from left to right, pushing and pressing, she covered the entire width of the backing, with no effect.

She said over her shoulder, "You are sure you didn't dream this?"

"Perhaps you have to say a magic word," Julie suggested.

Ben snorted. "And what did you say? 'I can't walk in these things.' Doesn't sound magic to me."

"Where exactly were you standing, Julie?"

The child took up a position outside the cupboard. "Then the heels went over and I fell forward. I tried to cling onto the clothes, but they gave way and I crashed against the back."

"But *where?*"

Julie looked doubtful. "About here, I think."

"Then why won't it open now?"

"I don't know. We couldn't get it to, either, the next time we tried."

"Well, have another go now. If it opened once, it'll do it again."

But despite their efforts, twenty minutes later the back remained implacably in position. Jan stepped out of the cupboard, face flushed and hair untidy from brushing against the clothes.

"It's not going to work," she said briskly, "and we've wasted quite enough time on it. If we don't hurry and collect our things, we'll be late for lunch."

"But I wanted to see the jewels," whined Julie.

"We'll come back and try again."

"But you do believe us, don't you, Mum?" Ben asked anxiously.

Jan hesitated. The wooden back gave weight to their story, but how could Julie's chance push have succeeded while all their concerted efforts failed? "I believe you think you saw something," she compromised. "What or how I don't know. In the meantime, just in *case* that was what interested the burglar, we won't mention this to anyone."

They nodded solemnly and followed her out of the room. It was with a sense of relief that she closed the door behind them.

That morning, Wood Street's report on Sinclair had been on Webb's desk, and after a quick glance at it, he buzzed for Jackson.

"Highly organized, by the look of it," he said. "He's built up a nice little circle of contacts—bank managers and suchlike—through whose services he can line his pockets."

"But how does it work, guv?"

"I imagine Rollo and the others get a list of investments Sinclair wants to push, and when their clients come for advice, they're gently nudged in the right direction. In return for which, Rollo and Co. get a handsome backhander. But his days are numbered; a report's gone to his Head Office—no doubt he'll be hearing from them."

"It sounds very dodgy. I thought bank managers were a cautious lot."

"There are exceptions to any rule, but I'd guess it seems fairly innocuous at first. They get a percentage of the commission—something like that. But then it escalates. If they bring in the big fish, they're suitably rewarded—lunch or dinner in the Big City, with optional extras."

"Like at The Commodore?"

"Precisely. And once they're in that deep, it's added protection against belated stirrings of conscience. Anyway, Marriott smelt a rat and started sniffing around."

"You reckon that's why he died?"

Webb sighed. "Could have been. At the very least, it's another line of inquiry to be followed through. God, Ken, I wish Stan Bates was mobile. We need all the help we can get on this one."

"Have you heard how he's going on, guv?"

"Not since Thursday. Which reminds me, I promised to look in again. In the meantime, though, I've prevailed on Court Lane to root out the other solicitors. We'll see what that brings forth. Oh, and permission from the Home Office is through on Peru. Evening flight from Heathrow tomorrow, so bring your case in to work. Just the bare essentials—we'll be issued with specialist gear on arrival. We'll check with Doc Pringle what jabs we should have. In the meantime, phone Mrs. Coverdale, will you Ken, and see if there's anything else we ought to know."

Jan returned from the phone and resumed her seat by the fire. Miles, who'd been invited for Sunday lunch, regarded her quizzically.

"You're looking very pensive. Not bad news, I hope?"

"No, just the police with last-minute queries on Peru. They're flying out tomorrow."

"Will they be able to contact them?" Lady Peel asked. "They could be deep in the jungle."

Miles laughed. "Believe me, if Webb's interested enough to go all that way, a bit of jungle's not going to stop him."

"But how can Edward help?" Jan demanded. "He's been away the whole time."

"We don't even know," Lady Peel said, "that it's Edward they wish to question."

"Rowena?" Jan stared at her. "I never thought of that. You think they might want to ask about the letter?"

"What letter?" Miles's voice was sharp, and they looked at him in surprise. Lady Peel explained about Sir Reginald's withdrawal.

"Ah, that explains it. Webb asked if I'd had one."

"But you haven't?"

Miles bent and stroked the cat on the rug. Her fur twitched in protest and she flicked her tail.

"No."

"He also mentioned a book your father might have written."

"That's right. Some nonsense about a schoolgirl magazine."

"They seem to believe it existed," Jan said.

"Then he must have destroyed it later." He stood up suddenly. "God, I'm sick of all this ferreting into our affairs. I'll be glad when it's over and they leave us in peace." He looked down at Jan. "You're not having much of a holiday, are you? Let me take you out to dinner, to make up for it. Mario's in Gloucester Street has a decent menu."

Jan said quickly, "That's kind of you, but I don't think—"

"Why not, my dear?" Lady Peel interrupted. "It's an excellent idea. Miles is right, this has been a most trying trip for you. Why not take the chance to relax for an evening? The children will be quite safe with Edith and me."

Any further protest would be embarrassing. Jan was aware of the amusement in Miles's gaze. Damn him! she thought impotently. Aloud, she said, "Then thank you. I'd enjoy that."

"Tomorrow suit you? I'll call for you at eight. Mondays are fairly quiet, there should be no problem getting a table."

Ken Jackson said, "I haven't any option, love. The guv says 'Jump,' and I jump. That's the way it is."

Millie shivered, and the baby she was holding stirred sleepily. She was in her dressing-gown, and the warm, domestic picture they presented emphasized the point she was making. "All the times we've sat here by the telly, me with my knitting and you in your slippers, watching people pitting themselves against the elements and taking terrible risks. And I've sipped my cocoa, thinking how lovely it was to be safe and snug at home. And now you'll be out there with them. Oh, Ken!"

"I shan't be in danger, love," he reassured her. "No more than going after a villain here in Shillingham. And as far as we know, Mr. Langley's not a villain anyway."

"He might have killed that man," Millie pointed out.

"Aye, and he might not, which is what we've got to find out. But he won't kill us, never fear. There'll be other people about, anyway, the lads who fly us out, and—and the Indians," he ended less certainly.

"Indians?" Millie's round eyes widened still further, and Jackson made a hasty substitution.

"Peruvians, then. The guides and people. And it will only take a few days anyway. Then I'll be back, and we can watch telly to our hearts' content."

She smiled, resting her cheek on the baby's fluffy red head. He smelt of warm milk and talcum powder. "Yes, of course. I know I'm being silly—it's just that it's so far away. Peru might as well be the moon, for all I know about it."

Jackson grinned. "I don't think even the governor will send me to the moon. Not till it gets its quota of criminals, anyway." He nodded towards the drowsy child. "Shall I take him back to his cot?"

"We'll give him another five minutes. We don't want him waking Tessa."

"It's some time since Mr. Webb saw his godson," Jackson commented. "We could ask him round one Sunday, when the case is wrapped up."

"That'd be lovely. Paul and Vicky'd enjoy it, too—Mr. Webb's very good with them. Pity he's no children of his own."

"I doubt if he misses them," Jackson said.

"My God!" exclaimed Alec Pringle the next morning. "What the hell are you going out there for?"

Webb grinned and winked at Jackson. "An exotic holiday, and to hell with crime? That what you're thinking? Not true, unfortunately. The sergeant and I have to penetrate the impenetrable, and we want to know what jabs are called for."

The police surgeon leant back in his chair. "This evening, you say? Left it a bit late, haven't you?" He was a tall, expatriate Scot, known for unfailing cheerfulness whatever the occasion. It was a trait which new recruits, initially shocked, quickly came to appreciate in a tough and stomach-turning world.

"No option, I'm afraid. The Home Office didn't pronounce till yesterday."

"Right, we'll see what we can do. Peru, you say. From what I remember, there are no required innoculations, but I'll check the chart. 'The King of Peru, who was Emperor too—' I always think of that. *Christopher Robin,* isn't it?" He was running his finger down the chart. "Aye, here we are. Nothing required, but I'd advise some protection. Your polio boosters are up to date, and I can give you one for typhoid. Hepatitis is easy—immediate protection on that one—and you'll need malaria tablets if you're going into the jungle. It's a bit late to start, but carry on taking them for six weeks. And that, my lads, is the best I can do for you. You'll have to get your yellow fever jab at Heathrow, so allow time before your flight."

"Ye gods! We'll be like a couple of pin-cushions!"

"This still the Chedbury case? Casting your nets wide, aren't you?"

Webb grinned. "The long arm of the law," he said.

It was as he was leaving his office en route to the airport that a phone call came through from Broadminster.

"Spider? Foggy Horn. Regarding that solicitor inquiry, I've got my lads' report here. Want me to summarize?"

Webb reached for paper and pen. "Please, Foggy."

"Here goes, then. First William Langley. You were right—he left letters for both his son and daughter. They're holding Edward Langley's till his return from Peru, but they didn't know Mrs. Coverdale was here, so hers was sent to Oz."

Webb whistled softly. "Now, that *is* interesting. They didn't happen to say what was in them, I suppose?"

"They haven't a clue. They were simply asked to deliver the sealed envelopes at the required time, and that's what they're doing."

"Three months after the survivor's death?"

"That's it."

"And the date they were deposited?"

"February, nineteen fifty-six."

"That figures. And Laurence Coady?"

"Even more interesting. He deposited a letter for his son at the same time, i.e. February fifty-six. But a year or so later, he also left a parcel with the same instructions. Again, they don't know what it contained, but it felt like a bundle of papers."

"His manuscript! So it *did* exist! And what happened to it?"

"Both it and the letter were delivered to Coady last week, by registered post. The GPO confirmed it."

"Did they, by Jove?" Webb said softly.

"You've already questioned him, I presume?"

"Oh yes, and naturally he denied all knowledge."

"Want us to have another word?"

Webb hesitated. He would have preferred to go back to Coady himself, but he'd be away for a week or more, and the man could be a killer. "Thanks, Foggy, I'd be grateful if you would."

Mario's restaurant went in for low lights and soft music, both of which Jan would willingly have dispensed with in Miles's company. They were seated with many flourishes at a corner table that was screened by plants from its nearest neighbours. Menus were produced, their selections made, and Miles ordered wine. Then he leant back in his chair, smiling across at her.

"Well, this is very pleasant. I'm glad of a chance to relax myself; I've been burning the midnight oil for the last week or so."

"On Buckhurst Grange?"

"Yes. It's coming along quite well. If you like, I'll drive you over one day, and you can have a look round. It's not officially open till Easter, but I can go whenever I want."

"That would be lovely, having seen your sketches."

"Which reminds me," he said casually, "on our day out, you mentioned a book of Sir Reginald's."

"Oh yes." Jan was not sure that she wanted to talk about it.

"You hinted there was something odd in it."

"It was probably nothing." She looked up at him, and came to a decision. Lately, there'd been so many things that puzzled her; perhaps Miles could provide some answers. In any case, it would be a relief to discuss them.

"It was a book called *Treasures of the Incas*, and there was a section on those that have never been recovered. Two were described in detail, the original Punchao and Cura Ocllo's emerald collar." She glanced up at him with a smile. "I'm not sure how much of this brushed off on you, but the Punchao was a sun image made of gold. Cura Ocllo was the wife of Manco Inca, who went into exile at Vilcabamba."

"And the collar?"

"It was said to be composed of nine emeralds, as large as quails' eggs."

"Nine emeralds. I see. Go on." His large, dark eyes were fixed on her face.

"Well, that's almost all. But what struck me as strange was that a large pencil bracket had been drawn in the margin, enclosing the whole page, and beside it was an exclamation mark."

He went on staring at her in silence.

"I'm sorry if you were expecting something more dramatic," she said, with an embarrassed little laugh. A waiter appeared and began to lay out their cutlery. The wine was produced, tasted, and pronounced satisfactory. When they were alone again, Jan cast around for some comment to break the growing silence between them.

"I don't know why I—" but he stopped her with a movement of his hand.

"You were right, Jan—it is very strange."

"Have you any idea what it means?"

"I believe I have, yes."

They were interrupted by the arrival of their first course. When it had been served, Jan looked at Miles expectantly. But he picked up his fork and began to eat in silence. Puzzled, she did the same. But after several minutes, when he still hadn't spoken, she burst out, "Well? Aren't you going to explain?"

"I'm sorry. I was wondering how to go about it. But since you told me about the book, I'll tell you something. Shortly before Sir Reginald died, I called round to inquire after him. I arrived at the same time as the vicar, and Mary wanted a word with him. She asked me if I'd take her place in the sick-room for a few minutes."

To Jan's frustration, the waiter approached again to remove their plates. She could have wished the service at Mario's had been less efficient.

"Yes?" she prompted, as he moved away.

"Well, he was tossing and turning and complaining about the sunlight, which was shining straight onto his face. I went to draw the curtains, and as I was doing so, he gave a strangled cry. I hurried back to the bed, wondering if I should call Mary, but he reached up and grabbed my hand, staring up into my face. And he said, 'You will do the right thing, won't you, Edward? Your father was right, we should never have kept it.' Then he fell back on the pillow and closed his eyes."

Jan found that her heart was thumping. "And that was all?"

"I said, 'Kept what?' and he muttered something that I couldn't catch."

"So what did you do?"

"Well, I didn't want to say anything to Mary. We all knew he was dying, and she was too upset to be questioned. But after the funeral I asked Edward and Rowena about it."

"And could they help?"

Miles smiled grimly. "They *could* have, but they didn't. At first, they tried to make out the old man had been rambling. Then Rowena flew off the handle and began ranting and raving about it being too early and she hadn't had time to think. And Edward did his stuffy act, pretending he didn't know what I was talking about. Not unnaturally, I lost my temper, and a lot of harsh words were said. It ended in an almighty row, since when I've been *persona non grata* at Rylands."

"But I don't understand. Why should they react like that?"

Miles was silent for a moment, and his next question when it came seemed the height of irrelevance. "Are you having your mail forwarded from Australia?"

Jan gazed at him blankly. "What?"

"Your mail. Is it being forwarded?"

"No, I didn't bother. There's not likely to be anything important. Why?"

"Because, my dear, something *very* important will be lying on your hall mat right now."

"What are you talking about?"

"A letter from your father."

She went very still. "You mean he really did write one?"

"Almost certainly. I received mine last week. It had been lodged with Father's solicitors, for delivery three months after Sir Reginald's death."

"So we were all left one?"

"That's right."

Jan felt the colour draining out of her face. "About the third expedition?"

He nodded. "Until mine arrived, I didn't know any more than you do. But yesterday, Mary said Sir Reginald had withdrawn his to Rowena after your father's death."

"And you think that's significant?"

"Oh, it's significant, all right. It means she knew the contents long before we did."

Jan said slowly, "You said yesterday that you hadn't had a letter."

"I know. I didn't want to discuss it in front of Mary."

"And did you also receive your father's book?"

He held her eyes for a moment. Then he said quietly, "Yes. I'm sorry I lied to you."

"You also lied to the police, which is more important."

"Not to me, it isn't. What my father wrote wasn't intended to be pawed over by the police."

Their plates were removed, their entrées served, and again they ate in silence. Then Jan said quietly, "Are you going to tell me what was in the letter?"

"Do you want me to?"

Did she? After all the wondering, now that the answer was within her reach, she was afraid to hear it. It must be momentous indeed, to have been kept secret for thirty years. Did she want to learn it from Miles, over a restaurant table? Or from her father, in words which had been carefully chosen for her alone?

"I'm not sure that I do. You must think me an idiot."

"Not at all. In some ways, I wish I didn't know, either."

"If I change my mind, will you tell me later?"

"Of course. But don't worry about it; your father wasn't in as deep as the others."

Their plates were removed and the dessert trolley wheeled across, but Jan's appetite had gone. The meal which was supposed to have offered a respite had failed abysmally.

Over coffee, Miles said, "I suppose you are going back to Australia? Permanently, I mean."

"There's nothing for me here."

"That's rather up to you."

Her mouth went dry. "All the children's friends are there. They're doing well at school."

"What about you?"

She shrugged. "It's been my home for fifteen years."

"You'll go ahead with a divorce?"

"I don't know." And suddenly, appallingly, she was crying. She reached blindly for her handbag. "Oh, Miles, I'm sorry! I don't know what's the matter with me."

"It's been an emotional evening, one way or another."

She was grateful that he made no attempt to comfort her. Nor, when they parted at Cajabamba, did he repeat his kiss.

Wearily she went upstairs and prepared for bed. Sleep was all she needed, she told herself. Things would be clearer in the morning.

But sleep would not come. Her mind revolved obsessively round the description in the book, Sir Reginald's words, the children's, till they jumbled together in a whirling, confusing spiral, latching onto each other completely out of context.

Should never have kept it. Jewels, shining in the cupboard. Nine flawless emeralds.

She sighed and turned over, and the words melded like a kaleidoscope coming together in a fresh pattern. Nine emeralds —brightly shining. Nine bright shiners.

Jan sat bolt upright, her eyes flying open. In her mind, she was back in the drawing-room at Rylands, with the children sorting out Christmas cards. And she remembered Julie's child-ish treble: "Nine for the Nine Bright Shiners." And the crash as Rowena, white-faced with shock, dropped the flower-vase. *The emeralds?* Was there some connection with them?

Think! she told herself fiercely. What exactly had Miles said about his visit to Cajabamba? That Sir Reginald had complained about the sun in his eyes, and he'd drawn the curtains. *But what were the old man's actual words?* Had he in fact been saying, "The Sun! The Sun!" And then, "We should never have kept it."

Had the three of them, on that portentous third expedition,

somehow found the missing treasure? Was that what lay behind the pencilled exclamation mark?

Jan got out of bed, slipped on her dressing-gown and started pacing the room. There was no sense in it. The men were respected explorers and archaeologists, not thieves. If they *had* found anything valuable, they'd have handed it to the authorities. How, in any case, could they have smuggled it out of the country? Yet there was something underhand about it. Miles had said: "Your father wasn't in as deep as the others."

She sat down at the dressing-table, her elbows on the cold glass. Suppose, just suppose, that they'd smuggled something out of Peru. What would they do with it? If they'd no legal right to it, it couldn't be insured or deposited in a bank. Where could it be hidden for safekeeping?

In the secret cupboard her father'd used for his war-time transmitters. That could have been why Edward and Rowena were told; they'd inherited Rylands, and Sir Reginald needed access.

Jan straightened, laying her palms flat on the glass and staring at her reflection. So perhaps it was true, what the children had said about a necklace rivalling the Crown Jewels. And the round, gold thing Ben had mentioned, which she'd taken to be a tray: could that conceivably be the priceless missing Punchao? Was it possible that her own children, at home in Rylands, had indeed found the lost treasure of the Incas?

It was over an hour later, when she was at last on the edge of sleep, that an even more startling thought came to her. There'd been nine green sequins on the dead man's jacket. The murderer, too, knew about the Nine Bright Shiners.

CHAPTER 12

It had been an exhausting flight, two European stop-overs followed by a change of plane at Caracas. Though they landed at Lima mid-morning local time, Webb and Jackson's interior clocks thought otherwise, and the plunge into summer after snowy Broadshire increased their disorientation.

They were met by a member of the British Embassy, who escorted them to the hotel where he'd booked them in. He was a pleasant, fresh-faced young man called Kevin Franks.

"I gather you're interested in Edward Langley?" he said in the car. "I hope he's not been blotting his copybook; he's quite a local hero out here."

"We only want to talk to him," Webb said. His left arm was throbbing and swollen after the injections, and he was anxious not to say too much till he could think more clearly.

"Pretty important talk, to bring you all this way!"

"Have you been able to trace him?"

"Yes, a plane went out from Cuzco when the message came through. He was in a pretty inaccessible place, though—a narrow ledge surrounded by forest. They'll have moved on, of course, by the time you get there, but you may well have to be winched down. And there are other complications," Franks added, almost apologetically. "Not only is it bandit country, it's also the centre of terrorist activity, a revolutionary outfit known as the *Sendero Luminoso*, or Shining Path. They're carrying on a permanent battle with the military."

"Great!" said Jackson under his breath. The last thing he fancied was being caught in the cross-fire out in the wilds somewhere. The brilliant sunshine hurt his eyes, and the scene outside the window seemed garish and unreal. He could do with a good kip, and hoped the governor felt the same.

The hotel was clean and unpretentious, and they each had a private bath. Jackson, whose ideas of Peru were even less informed than Webb's, was grateful for small mercies.

"I suggest you have a quiet afternoon," Franks was saying. "Then my wife and I would be pleased if you'd dine with us."

"That's kind of you. You mentioned Cuzco; presumably that's our starting point when we set out to see Langley. How far is it from here?"

"Oh, a fair way—right up in the Andes. We've booked you on the midday flight tomorrow."

Webb raised his eyebrows. "Flight?"

"Since you're in a hurry, it's much the quickest way. The journey can take a couple of days by bus or train, not to mention the possibility of being stopped by *los terroristas,* or police looking for them. But you'll have to take things easy when you get there. The dreaded altitude sickness is no respecter of persons." He hesitated. "Is there anything you'd like to see while you're in Lima?"

Webb gave him a tired grin. "At the moment, the inside of this room looks pretty good to me!"

"Fine, I think that's very wise. Incidentally, if you do go out, watch out for pick-pockets. We've a terrible problem here with thieving of all kinds. I'd advise keeping your ticket, passport and money with you the whole time, preferably somewhere inaccessible.

"Well, if there's nothing else at the moment, I'll leave you to have a rest. When you're ready for lunch, there's a good choice of restaurants nearby, or the hotel dining-room's quite reasonable, if you'd prefer that."

Webb nodded his thanks, but food was the last thing on his mind. He wanted peace and quiet to get his bearings, and when Franks had left them and Jackson gone to his own room, he took out the sketches he'd made of the people in the case. They seemed a long way away now, Miles Coady, Tony Rollo and

Lady Peel. He hoped that by the time he saw them again in the flesh, he would know for certain who the murderer was.

That day had the unreality of a dream. Jet-lag and general tiredness blended impressions into a confused medley of heat and colour, of dusty shanty towns and wide plazas, of street stalls selling traditional cheese-filled pastries, and the culture-shock of a Kentucky Fried Chicken.

When the Franks collected them that evening, they were given a quick tour round the old city—the squat cathedral, the Museum of the Inquisition with its classical columns, and the superb Torre Tagle Palace, before driving down broad, tree-lined Avenida Arequipa to the modern centre of Miraflores, where they were to dine.

"It's too bad you're not here longer," Lucy Franks told them. "We'd enjoy showing you round."

Webb made some politic reply. Had his time been his own, he would indeed have welcomed the chance to look at the ancient ceramics and weavings the Franks spoke of, and the display of modern Peruvian art. But he was on business, and although this enforced stop-over in Lima was both sensible and necessary, he was now filled with impatience to track down Langley.

But when the Franks left them at their hotel, they repeated their warning about height sickness. "The standard advice when you get to Cuzco is to take it very easy for at least three days. The altitude plays havoc with the metabolism, and if you're not careful, *soroche* can make you seriously ill. It doesn't affect every-one, but the way to avoid it is to take plenty of rest, and eat only light meals." Sensing Webb's impatience, Kevin Franks smiled. "Edward Langley will still be there when you're ready for him," he said.

To the detectives' relief, both of them were spared the more severe effects of *soroche*. The hour's flight to Cuzco had brought them to another world, a bustling, busy little city on the top of the world, whose streets were thronged with Quechuan Indians in their colourful ponchos and woollen hats.

They were met by members of Langley's rear party, whom Franks had contacted on their behalf. Rob Jeffries, a tall blond man, was naturally concerned.

"We weren't given any details, Chief Inspector. It's nothing serious, is it?"

"Serious enough. Mr. Langley's housekeeper was murdered last week," Webb replied.

"Well, I'm sorry to hear that, but as you know, Edward and Rowena have been here for over two weeks. I don't see how they can help you."

"Nor do I, Mr. Jeffries, but I assure you I do need to speak to them. I gather they're in the jungle somewhere?"

"That's right. They'll be between Chaullay and Cajabamba. They phoned on Friday before leaving Machu Picchu, but we've no way of contacting them now, other than by dropping a message with supplies. Radios don't function in the rain forests."

"Where are they actually making for?"

"Cajabamba, which, as you may know, their fathers discovered in nineteen-fifty. At the moment there's a lot of guerrilla activity in the area; they had to get written permission from the *prefecto* before setting out, and it was only given because they're such celebrities over here."

"So they don't know we're on our way?"

"No." Jeffries looked worried again. "Look, I do hope it won't be necessary to abort the trip. A hell of a lot of planning and expense has gone into it."

"I hope not, too," Webb said implacably. "I believe you've kindly offered to kit us out?"

"That's right. Sleeping bags, mess tins and waterproofs— we're in the rainy season, as you may have noticed. You've got a supply of malaria tablets, I take it?"

"Yes, we've been on them for a couple of days. That was all the notice we had."

"Fine. We've made an appointment for you to see the Secret Police in the morning—always best to keep in with them—and there's a chopper standing by when you're ready. But do give yourselves a couple of days to get acclimatized. Believe me, it'll be time well spent."

Webb had expected the jungle to be flat, but from the valley floor, dense forests rose steeply, clinging to precipitous mountainsides and clothing them in green. From time to time, they flew over isolated villages in clearings among the trees—a blue-walled school, a few scattered houses.

"There they are," the man beside them said suddenly. "They've made good progress since Sunday—I was beginning to think we might have missed them."

Webb leant sideways and peered out of the window. Below, in a small clearing, he could see a couple of tents, a couple of mules, and two waterproofed figures staring up at them.

"Sorry we can't make a landing—this is about as low as we can get. All set?"

Webb glanced at Jackson's white face. "As set as we'll ever be."

"OK. We'll pick you up at the same time tomorrow."

By the time Jackson had joined Webb on the ground, Edward Langley was waiting for them. The face under the hood of the waterproof poncho could, at first sight, have been Marriott's, resurrected from the mortuary slab. Though Webb had expected the likeness, it was oddly unnerving.

"Mr. Langley?" (A touch of the Dr. Livingstones, he thought with wry amusement.)

"Yes. Who the hell are you?"

Webb started to speak, but the noise of the helicopter drowned his voice. Langley took his arm, and beckoning to Jackson, led them into the larger tent. Rowena Langley was waiting inside.

"Who are you? What do you want?"

"Chief Inspector Webb and Sergeant Jackson, ma'am, Shillingham CID."

"*Shillingham?*" She spun to face her husband. "That damned sister of yours! I said it was a risk, having her over, but no, you felt sorry for her. And this is how she repays us!"

"Rowena! Please!" Langley turned to Webb. "Perhaps you'd tell us your business, Chief Inspector."

Again his wife broke in. "God, isn't it obvious? She's been talking to Miles—he'll have got his letter by now." She faced Webb defiantly. "We were going to hand them over, for God's sake, but we couldn't do anything while my father was alive. As it is, the scandal could kill Mother."

"Hand what over, ma'am?"

"The treasure, of course." She stopped abruptly, and he saw the first doubt in her eyes, the fear that she'd needlessly incriminated herself.

"That they brought back from the fifty-five expedition?" Webb asked, with magnificent aplomb, and Jackson glanced at him admiringly. You had to hand it to the governor. *Treasure?* What the hell was she on about?

Rowena let out her breath. "So you do know about it. I was beginning to wonder if I'd spoken out of turn."

"As a matter of fact, ma'am, we didn't, though we'd have got there soon enough. We've come to see you—or at least your husband—on a different matter."

Edward Langley said quickly, "It isn't Janis, is it, or one of the children? Nothing's happened to them?"

"Not to them, no. But quite a bit's been happening since you left Broadshire, sir."

"Look, I imagine you'll be here for some time. You might as well make yourselves comfortable. Take off your waterproofs, for a start, and unroll your sleeping bags. They make for softer sitting than the ground."

He produced some bottles of *chicha* maize beer and they all settled themselves, while the continuous dripping of rain on the roof of the tent made a rhythmic background to their conversation. It was, Webb thought, the weirdest interview he'd ever conducted, both in content and location. If someone had told him, a week ago, that he'd be sitting with Jackson in the middle of the Peruvian jungle—

From the corner of his eye, he saw that Ken had extracted his notebook. Good lad. Front room in Shillingham, or South

American rain forest, a murder inquiry was still a murder inquiry. He took a sip of beer, and began his questioning.

"Did you know a man called Guy Marriott, sir?"

"No, why?"

It seemed, Webb thought wearily, that no one would ever admit to knowing Marriott. "Because he was found dead last week, with your wallet in his pocket."

"So that's what happened to it. It was stolen from the squash club a couple of months back."

"Yes, sir, we know about that. But he was also dressed in a shabby jacket which didn't belong to him, with nine green sequins on its lapel."

He glanced at Rowena Langley. She had opened her mouth, but closed it again.

"And there was a bandage on his arm, though no sign of injury. Do those things convey anything to you, sir?"

It was Rowena who answered. "The Nine Bright Shiners," she said.

Langley was gazing at the ground in front of him. "That's what my wife christened the collar."

"What collar would that be, sir?"

Langley looked up. "You mean you really don't know? That's not why you're here?"

"It might well be, sir, but only indirectly. I'm sorry to tell you that last week your housekeeper, Mrs. Carr, was also murdered."

"Lily? My God, how?"

"It seems she disturbed a burglar. Your sister and the children were in London for the day."

"And they found her? How ghastly for them. Poor old Lily." He was silent for a moment. Then he said, "Was her death connected with that chap Marriott? Who was he, by the way?"

"A journalist, from London."

"Was he after the treasure?"

"We haven't established that yet, but it seems likely." Webb paused. "Have you any thoughts on the bandage, sir?"

"None whatever. Presumably he'd sprained his arm."

"The pathologist said it was put on after death. That ring a bell, sir? A tight bandage put on after death?"

"Are you trying to say it represented a mummy? That's rather a long shot, isn't it?"

"Maybe, but it occurred to both your sister and Mr. Coady."

Langley shrugged. "Taken in conjunction with the sequins and wallet, it's possible someone was pointing the finger at me. Though God knows, it would have been simpler to approach me direct. But if this Marriott was after *me*, who was after him?"

"He was actually killed before Christmas, on or about the eighteenth of December."

"While I was still around? Is that what you're getting at?"

"You could have caught him with your wallet, lost your temper and killed him accidentally."

"I could have, but I didn't. Was the money still in it?"

"Yes."

"Odd, that. Several other wallets were pinched the same day, but they turned up later, with nothing missing. Why should mine be singled out for special treatment? He took my diary, too, which—"

"Your diary?" Webb broke in sharply. "I didn't know that."

Langley looked surprised. "It was hardly worth reporting, just an inconvenience."

"Was anyone else's taken?"

"I didn't ask. We were only concerned about the wallets."

"I wish I'd known this. It could have opened up the line of inquiry."

But Langley wasn't interested in the diary. "If my wallet was taken to throw suspicion on me, why wait so long before using it?"

"And why should he *want* to throw suspicion on you?"

Langley's eyes fell. "We keep coming back to the treasure, don't we?"

"Suppose, sir, you tell us about that expedition of your father's. It might help to clear things up."

"That's why we're here now, as a matter of fact," Langley said reflectively. "One last visit while we're still welcome guests. The weather's not ideal, but we had to come."

He shifted his position and took a long draught of beer, wiping his mouth with the back of his hand. On the canvas above them, the rain kept up its remorseless patter, and a rumble of thunder rolled along the valley wall.

"All right—it'll be a relief to get it over. Here goes then: the trip had been plagued with difficulties from the outset. Supplies were held up, which delayed the start of it, and soon afterwards my father went down with some virulent bug. They kept hoping he'd shake it off, but he got steadily worse, and finally had to be air-lifted to hospital. So what happened initially concerned only my wife's father and Coady."

"Go on, sir."

"Well, the aim of the expedition was to trace the last living descendants of Manco Inca. It had been thought the line had died out, but Coady'd discovered there were a couple of members living in a remote mountain village not far from here. So he and Sir Reginald set out to find them. To cut a long story short, they did find the village, and the man, José Quispe Tupac, but only just in time. He was dying, and what was worrying him most was that having no children, he was the last of his line.

"When he realized his visitors were the men who'd discovered Cajabamba, he became very excited and instructed his wife to dig in the hard mud floor in the corner of the cabin. After some time, she managed to extract a dirty old blanket, wrapped round something."

Langley looked up and met Webb's eyes. "It contained a priceless emerald collar which had belonged to his ancestor Cura Ocllo, Manco's sister-queen. And, even more startling, the original Punchao, a golden image of the sun containing the powdered hearts of dead Incas, which was their most treasured possession."

Webb wondered fleetingly how Jackson had spelt "Cura Ocllo." But Langley was continuing. "These fantastic works of art were placed in the dying man's hands, and with great ceremony he then passed them over to Coady, entrusting him to take them to the Sun Temple at Pachácamac. This, of course, had been violated at the time of the conquest, and it seemed incredible he didn't know that. Perhaps he just didn't want to, because, though they did their best to explain, he refused to listen. To him, it was still the most sacred of places, and nowhere else would do. When the men tried to argue with him, he became very agitated and made them swear not to hand the treasures to the government. That's not surprising; Indians generally have little faith in the Peruvian government. Perhaps they regard it as their conquerors' natural successor.

"Anyway, all this excitement was apparently too much for him, and he lapsed into a coma shortly afterwards. Peel and Coady took the wife to one side and tried to explain to her, but she was terrified of being held responsible for the treasure, and begged them to take it. She said her husband would die happy, knowing it was safe."

Langley looked across at Webb. "All right," he challenged him, "what would you have done?"

"I don't know, sir. The point is, what did they do?"

"Well, they couldn't leave it there. The woman was weeping and beseeching them to take it. She wrapped it up in the blanket again, and pushed it into their hands."

"Just a minute," Webb interrupted. "How big was that idol thing? It'd be pretty heavy, surely?"

"Surprisingly, no. It only weighs about five pounds—they'd no difficulty carrying it. So they made their way back to Cuzco, endlessly discussing what they should do.

"My father, meanwhile, had been moved down to Lima, to assist his breathing. He was still extremely weak, and was to be flown home on a stretcher. That seemed to offer the best chance of getting the things out of the country, so just before the flight, Coady pushed them under his blankets. Father'd no idea what was going on—he was barely conscious—and since he went straight from hospital to the airport, he wasn't checked through customs. It was the same when they landed at home. And Peel extracted the treasures before he was taken to the Royal Broadshire."

"As simple as that," Webb said.

"Believe me, Chief Inspector, there was nothing simple about it. Those jewels changed the lives of all three men. When my father was well enough, Peel and Coady told him the story. Not having been there, he was horrified at what they'd done. But the other two had given their word to a dying man, and felt they couldn't go back on it."

"They could have told the British Government."

"Who'd have been bound to return the treasure to Peru. They didn't want a diplomatic incident on their hands. Finally, they decided to keep it hidden until all three of them were dead, leaving a posthumous letter with a full explanation to their children, who would be free to decide as they chose."

"But Sir Reginald withdrew his."

"Ah, you know about that. It was principally because the jewels were hidden at Rylands, but also, I suspect, because he was very close to my wife, and she accompanied him on several expeditions. It would have been asking too much of human nature to expect him not to confide in her."

Webb remembered Lady Peel. "Did he also confide in his wife?"

"No, and that was something all three men regretted. They explained in the letter that it was too much of a burden to place on their wives, but the real reason was Isabelle Coady. She was a neurotic woman, unbalanced and hardly the type to entrust with such a secret. And since she obviously couldn't be told, my father and Sir Reginald thought it unfair to tell their own wives."

So Lady Peel had spoken the truth. Obscurely, Webb was glad of that.

"Well, sir, it's quite a story, but I'm not sure it gets us much further. I still can't see any connection with Marriott, unless, as you say, he was after the treasure."

"But on reflection, he couldn't have been. At the time of his death, the only people who knew about it were my wife and myself."

"But Edward," Rowena interrupted, "Miles had his suspicions, didn't he?" She turned to Webb. "He visited Father just before he died, when he was rambling a bit. He must have mentioned the Nine Bright Shiners, because after the funeral Miles came and asked us about them. I thought we'd managed to fob him off, though there was an unpleasant scene. Even so, I'm sure he didn't know what the Shiners were."

Webb felt a prickle of excitement. "Mrs. Coverdale's letter was sent to Australia," he said thoughtfully, "but Coady received his as instructed. The post office confirmed it. He also received a parcel left by his father. Did you know Laurence Coady had written a book about the expedition?"

"We most certainly did not."

"They were both delivered by registered post last Wednesday, the day Mrs. Carr was killed."

The Langleys stared at him, shock in their faces. "My God, you think Miles killed Lily?"

"Suppose he read the letter, flicked through his father's manuscript, and, possibly knowing Mrs. Coverdale was out for the day, decided to look for the jewels."

"But why?" Rowena broke in. "We'd no intention of hanging onto them. When we got back, and before Janis left, we were going to have a discussion about them."

"Why didn't you discuss it when your father died?"

"Because we wanted them to hear the story from their fathers' letters first. The three-month interval was to ensure that nothing rash was decided in the aftermath of grief or shock, and it seemed sensible to stick to that."

"I *can't* believe Miles killed Lily," Edward said.

Webb could. "We assumed she'd been killed because she disturbed the burglar. Perhaps it was because she recognized him. However, the most damning evidence against Coady is the sequins on the jacket. From what you say, no one else could have known about the emeralds."

There was a long silence, while they all thought over what had been said and its possible implications. Then Langley said resignedly, "We'll come back with you, of course. We couldn't carry on here as if nothing had happened."

"I'd appreciate that, sir. The disposal of the jewels isn't my problem, thank goodness, but clearly I'll have to pass on the information. I'd just be much happier if we could see where Marriott fitted into all this."

In fact, the missing link had already been supplied. Two days earlier and some six thousand miles away, the telephone had rung in Broadminster police station.

"My name is Colin Plaidy," came a crisp voice over the line. "I'd like to speak to the officer in charge of the Marriott case."

CHAPTER 13

The day after their dinner together, Jan tried without success to telephone Miles. Her mind was still churning, but in the clear light of morning, she discounted some of her wilder imaginings. Above all, she needed to learn the contents of Laurence Coady's letter. If it confirmed that the jewels were at Rylands, a decision would have to be taken. They couldn't go to the police without consulting Edward, but a guard of some sort should be put on the house. The burglar might be more successful at a second attempt.

Why, oh why hadn't she let Miles tell her about the letter? she thought despairingly, as the answer-phone again came into operation. Unwilling to leave yet another message, she replaced the receiver and returned to the drawing-room, where Lady Peel was embroidering and the children engrossed in a film on television.

"I'm just slipping out for a while," she said. "I shan't be long." Lady Peel nodded, the children took no notice. She let herself quietly out of the house, tightening her belt as the cold wind tore at her coat. The snow was vanishing fast, and white clouds raced over a clear blue sky.

The Chief Inspector would have arrived in Lima by now. Why had he really gone all that way? Because he suspected Edward, if not of murder, of a serious crime? And *was* it Edward that the murdered man came to see?

The Rylands key was still in her handbag, and she made her way there without conscious thought. It was strange to be alone in the house that held so many ghosts for her, one of them sadly recent. Like a ghost herself, she moved restlessly from room to room. In the library, the jigsaw that the children had been playing with the day they went to London still lay on the table. She wished uselessly that she could turn the clock back. But how far? To before Lily's death? Guy Marriott's? Roger's defection?

She turned and half ran from the room and up the stairs. Bracing herself, she again entered her half-brother's bedroom and went to the wardrobe. But several minutes' sustained pressing and prodding produced no effect whatever. The wardrobe was preserving its secret.

Miles phoned at nine o'clock that evening. With a glance over her shoulder, Jan spoke quickly and quietly. "Miles, I must see you as soon as possible. I think I've discovered what Sir Reginald meant, and the meaning of the pencil marks, but I need to know what was in your father's letter."

"No problem about that. What changed your mind?"

Another glance confirmed there was no one within earshot. "I think I know where they are."

There was a long silence. Then he said, "They?"

"You know what I mean."

"And where are they?" he asked softly.

"At Rylands. The children found them, but I didn't realize."

"Now you *have* aroused my curiosity. Very well, I'll meet you there in the morning. Ten o'clock? But Jan—better not to say where you're going. Just in case."

He phoned again the next morning. "Sorry to be a nuisance, but could I ask a favour? I left a sketch there on Sunday, and I want to get it in the post before midday. Could you possibly send the children round with it? Then I can put it into an envelope, and post it on the way to Rylands."

She hesitated. "I'm not sure they remember the way."

"Of course they do. It's a sketch of the rose-garden at Buckhurst—I brought it to show Mary, and must have left it on the table by the window."

"All right, I'll see if I can find it."

"Thanks so much. If they leave straight away, we can still be at Rylands by ten o'clock."

The sketch was where he'd said. Jan handed it to Ben, instructing him to keep it flat. "Can you find your way to the Mews?"

"Of course—it's easy."

"Well, be careful, especially crossing roads, and don't talk to anyone on the way. I'll see you at Rylands in about half an hour."

But when Miles arrived at the house, he was alone.

Jan had the door open before he reached the steps. "Where are the children?" she demanded urgently. "Didn't they arrive? They left—"

"Hush!" He put his hand on her arm with a laugh. "Don't panic, mother hen. Of course they arrived, they're perfectly safe."

"Then where are they?"

"I gave them fifty pence for bringing the sketch, so they stopped off in Monks' Walk to buy sweets."

"But you should have waited for them." She was peering past him down the road.

"I was impatient to hear your news. Where are the jewels?"

"Could I see the letter before I show you?"

"It's here." He almost thrust it into her hand.

With a last glance up the road she closed the door, leaving it on the latch, and went into the library. Miles followed her with barely concealed impatience, watching her face as she read. The information in the letter was much as Webb would hear from Edward, but its tone was bitter, that of a man who felt wronged.

"The hidey-hole at Rylands is the best we could come up with," it ended, "but William's not happy about it. He refuses to take sole responsibility, which is why we and the Peels had to move to Broadminster. In any case, not having met Quispe Tupac, he doesn't feel so committed, and keeps saying we should hand it over.

"The truth is, those artefacts have soured our friendship. It was I who traced Quispe Tupac, and into my hands that he put the treasure, but since we reached home, I've been pushed aside. William, apart from housing them, has opted out, and Reggie's left in the limelight, which suits him very well. He's always giving lectures and appearing on TV, and though he's planning another trip, he hasn't asked me to join him. Yet it was I who introduced them to Peru!

"Still, to tell the truth, I've lost the stomach for it, specially since your mother died. All the same, I'm determined you'll know the true story some day, which is why I'm writing a book about it. Then you can make your own judgement."

Jan folded the letter and handed it back. At least it explained the ambivalence of the men's position regarding the jewels. That much, she registered with relief; but the overwhelming ramifications, the confirmation of her wild guess that the treasure was indeed upstairs, were too complex to grasp. For the moment, she was more concerned with the children's non-arrival. She glanced anxiously out of the window. "I wonder what's keeping them."

"For God's sake—they won't be long!" Miles burst out impatiently. "Look, don't keep me in suspense. Where are the jewels?"

"Behind the wardrobe in Edward's room, but it won't open. We've all been trying."

"Show me."

She led the way upstairs. "Julie was trying on Rowena's shoes and lost her balance. She fell forward into the wardrobe, knocking against the back of it, and it came open. But though we've pressed over the whole area, we can't make it move."

"Where was she standing?"

"Just here."

"So if she fell forward, she'd have knocked the wood about—here." He bent down, gave it a sharp tap, and the partition slid smoothly aside. Jan gasped and clutched at his shoulder. In the small space hollowed out of the wall stood a table, on which was a display model of a woman's head and shoulders; and clasped round the throat was the most beautiful necklace Jan had ever seen. Nine great emeralds sparkled in the light, living green fire against the dead polystyrene skin. And in front of them, their equal in splendour, lay the legendary sun idol, its encircling medallions so dazzling that the eye couldn't focus on the image itself.

Miles was still bending forward with his hand on the partition, but as he straightened, it began to slide shut.

"Wedge it open," Jan said quickly. "Or we might have the same trouble again."

"You must have been trying too high up." His voice was light and breathless. "It's an added safeguard, having the spring low down and not at the height you'd normally press. What incredible luck, that she fell at precisely the right level." He took the dressing-stool she handed him, and wedged open the space. Then he stood back beside her, gazing inside.

"I tried to imagine them." His voice was shaking. "But I never dreamt they'd be like this. What would you say they're worth?"

"It's impossible to put a price on them."

"Don't you believe it." The exultant note in his voice sent a shiver down her spine. He drew a deep breath and slowly released it. "Treasure-trove, right in front of our eyes. Think of it —the Sun Idol and the Nine Bright Shiners."

Jan glanced at him in surprise. "How d'you know they're called that?"

He blinked, interrupted in his euphoria. "Ah, you've caught me out there. The truth is, I didn't repeat everything Sir Reginald told me. He *did* answer, when I asked what he shouldn't have kept. He said, 'The Sun, of course, and the Nine Bright Shiners.' And when I looked blank, he added testily, 'The emeralds, boy, the emeralds.' "

Jan said clearly, "The murderer knew about them, too."

There was a silence, filled with the deafening sound of her heartbeats. God, what had she *said?* What had she *meant? And what had he done with the children?* Quite suddenly, their absence took on a new dimension of fear.

She spun to face him, only half-registering the knife which had materialized in his hand. "For God's sake, Miles, where are the children? Tell me the truth."

His mind on other things, it took him a moment to answer her. "They're safe enough. For the present."

"It was a trick, wasn't it? You weren't in any hurry for the sketch. Why did you do it?"

"As a form of insurance. Which, it appears, may well be necessary."

She fought to steady her voice, swallow the heartbeats which fluttered in her throat. "You swear you haven't harmed them?"

He was losing patience with her. "For God's sake, I've said they're all right. Whether they remain all right depends on you."

She whispered, "What do you want me to do?"

"I need to think. I hadn't included you in my plans, and there's too much at stake to take risks." He waved the knife at the nearer bed. "Sit down, while I work it out." He followed her, and they sat together on the cream, flowered duvet.

He must have locked them up somewhere. A cupboard in his house? His garage? How could she let someone know where they were? They'd be terrified. Please let it be true, that he hadn't hurt them. Oh God, how could she have let them go alone?

Miles was fingering the blade, his eyes on its lethal point. Across the room, they had a clear view into the secret cupboard, with its priceless contents. How many people, through the centuries, had killed to gain possession of them? Miles was just one more at the end of the line.

He said reasoningly, "They're mine by right, as my father's heir. You and Edward have no claim to them; your father was in hospital when they were found. And it wasn't Sir Reginald who traced Quispe Tupac. Rowena's not getting her hands on them again."

She said gently, "But Miles, they won't be any use to you. You can't sell them."

"Not as they are, of course. I'll take a lead from the Spaniards —melt down the gold and break up the necklace. Any one of those stones could be worth a million. And I have contacts. There'll be no problem."

Aghast, she stammered, "But you can't *destroy* them! Your father risked everything for them!"

"Look, I'm not interested in bloody Incas—I never have been. All that matters is what they're worth to *me*. Edward and Rowena may have other plans, but they're immaterial now."

There was no hope of rescue; he'd instructed her to tell no one she was coming here. Only the children knew, and they'd been taken hostage. She was completely on her own; her life and theirs depended on her quick thinking.

She stole a sideways glance at him, and saw to her amazement that he was smiling. He was pleased with himself, well satisfied with the way things had gone. Could that be her chance, to play on his vanity? She'd heard it was a common weakness in murderers.

With an effort, she said, "How did Marriott find out?"

His smile broadened. "He didn't. The police were on completely the wrong track. Marriott's death had nothing to do with either Edward or the treasure."

She said weakly, "Then why—"

"Did I kill him? Because he was going to print a story which would have destroyed my career."

"What story?" If she could keep him talking, some idea might come to her.

He shrugged. "I'd been unwise enough to pass someone else's work off as my own. When I was doing the Stately Homes series, I came across a folio of drawings under a pile of papers in an attic. They were exquisite—a series of eighteenth-century interiors, every detail meticulously observed. I made some discreet inquiries, and the owner clearly knew nothing about them, so I reasoned he wouldn't miss them. As it happened, I'd been commissioned for something very similar, and the deadline was fast approaching. So I traced the drawings, and slipped those in instead. Not surprisingly, they were extremely well received, and brought me a lot of publicity. It was on the strength of them that I got the Buckhurst commission."

"And Guy Marriott found out?"

"Yes, God knows how. He came down to see me. In fact the first time I saw you, in Monks' Walk, I was on my way to meet him."

"And what did he say?"

"Asked if I'd any comment on certain allegations he'd received. He wouldn't tell me who'd made them. I denied everything, naturally, but he wasn't fooled. After a lot of arguing, he said, 'Well, Mr. Coady, I'm going ahead with the story. You're free to sue us, but I doubt if you will.' I tried to talk him round then. Damn it, it was only a story to him, but for me it'd be disaster. I even offered him money, but he wouldn't budge. So I'd no choice."

Jan said aridly, "What did you do?"

"Cracked him over the head when he wasn't looking, and finished him off in the bath."

She felt the strands of nightmare closing over her. On the fringes of memory were Lady Peel's words about his mother. "But what about the jacket and sequins?" she asked. "And the wallet? Where did they fit in?"

He gave a brief laugh. "That's another story. They were in my cupboard, so I simply—"

"But why?" Jan interrupted. "What on earth were they doing in your cupboard?" A part of her mind was genuinely curious; it was a puzzle she'd been living with for ten days. But the main part was simply encouraging his boasting, waiting for a moment's inattention. Yet if her chance came, where could she run to? The en-suite bathroom was the nearest door with a lock, but if he were desperate enough, he could break it down. And the window was at the back of the house; she wouldn't be able to attract attention.

He was saying, "That was what confused the police. They were looking for a link-up, and there wasn't one. The wallet business goes back to my row with Edward and Rowena. I was determined to find out the truth, and I reasoned that if there *were* any jewels, they'd be in a safe-deposit box somewhere. It was more than likely Edward'd have a note of the number, in his diary or wallet, so I pinched them, together with my own wallet and a few others to deflect suspicion—you were right there. But unfortunately, they were no help.

"By this time it was the beginning of November, and the kids were going round collecting money for Guy Fawkes Day. So I decided to play a trick on Edward, and work off my spleen by making a guy of him. All right, it was childish, but in my present mood it appealed to me. I'd put his wallet in the guy's pocket for identification, and sew nine green sequins on the jacket. Then he'd know I was on to him.''

"And what were you going to do with it?''

"I hadn't decided. Perhaps leave it on the Green, or even in front of the police station. The idea was to embarrass him, that's all. I didn't expect anyone else to see the significance.

"So I bought some old clothes from a jumble sale, painted a face on a football, and assembled the thing. At which stage, I discovered he and Rowena had gone to Scotland for the week. There was no point in going through with it if he was away, so I put the dummy at the back of a cupboard and forgot about it.

"What happened next was pure coincidence. When Marriott arrived and I opened the door to him, the sun was in my eyes and I thought for a moment it was Edward. I said something like, 'I'm sorry—I thought you were someone else.'

"And he said, 'I'm always being told that. People say I look like that explorer chap on the telly.'

"That was the first thing. Then, when he was dead, I had to decide what to do with the body. I couldn't cart it round in its wet clothes, leaving a trail of water behind me. So I started to strip him, and as I pulled off his jacket, I noticed an envelope sticking out of a pocket. It was addressed to Guy Marriott. I hadn't registered his first name before, but the word 'Guy' leapt out at me, and I remembered the dummy in the cupboard. It struck me that it wasn't too late to play the trick on Edward, and since Marriott had a look of him, it would be even more effective."

He was talking more to himself than to Jan, still with that chilling satisfaction at his ingenuity.

"Mary had told me once there were mummies in Peru, so to hammer the point home, I tied a bandage round his arm. Then I wrapped him in a bin-bag so he'd leave no trace in the car, and drove up to Chedbury."

"Why Chedbury?" The question was simply to prolong his talking. She daren't think what would happen when he stopped.

"Partly to confuse the issue, partly because it was a quiet place to dump him. I did stop earlier, but a lorry with blazing head-lamps came round the corner just as I was opening the boot. It was a near thing, so I didn't take any more chances."

Playing on his vanity, Jan said, "How clever of you. Not many people could have thought clearly at such a time."

He nodded in agreement. "All the same, a body's very different from a dummy. If I'd had time to think it through, I wouldn't have used the wallet—it was too close to home. In any case, the plan misfired yet again; because of the tree, by the time the body was discovered Edward wasn't here to be embarrassed." He smiled grimly. "I don't mind telling you I'd some nasty moments when the police made the link with Peru. I hadn't expected that—I suppose you pointed it out."

Jan searched desperately for more questions. "What about Lily?"

"That was unfortunate. I'd received the letter and book that morning, and I knew you were in London. Having had all my suspicions about the treasure confirmed, I just *had* to see if I could find it."

"So you got in through the window Ben left open, and Lily heard you."

"It's almost directly over the kitchen. It never occurred to me she'd be there. And of course, once she found me in the study opening drawers—" He shrugged.

Keep talking. Oh God, what could she say? What could she *do?* Time was running out.

"I didn't want to kill her," Miles was continuing, and a petulant note had crept into his voice. "And I don't want to kill you, either. It's a pity you didn't stay safely in Australia."

Rigid with fear, Jan could only agree. "Let the children go, and I'll do anything you want!" she promised wildly.

He smiled. How had she ever thought him attractive? "But once they're free, there's nothing to hold you to that. You're in no position to bargain."

"Look, you said they were your insurance, and they are. I'll help you get away, if you'll tell me where they are."

"I'm sorry. You see, you're the only one who knows I did it."

"Exactly! Whereas if you kill me and disappear, *everyone* will know!"

He stood up and turned to face her, still fingering the blade. She realized sickly that only half of him wanted to spare her; the other half was excited by the thought of the knife. And as she watched him, the decision crystallized in his eyes, and she knew that she'd lost.

If she hurled herself sideways, dashed for the bathroom? With glazed eyes she watched him raise his arm. And a voice from the doorway said incredulously, "What the bloody hell's going on?"

"*Roger!*"

As the cry broke from her, Miles spun round, and in the same second Jan darted towards him, knocked the knife out of his hand and kicked it under the bed. Then, as Miles still stood in shock, Roger's fist made contact with his jaw and he fell heavily to the floor. Without thought, Jan hurled herself into her husband's arms.

CHAPTER 14

It was only when the children had been found in Miles's garage, gagged and bound but otherwise unharmed, that Jan questioned Roger about his opportune arrival.

"Mother phoned and told me what was happening," he explained. "There was a business trip in the offing, so I brought it forward and flew straight over. By the way, I collected these from the house." He felt in his pocket and handed her a pile of letters. The one on top was from the Broadminster solicitors.

Seeing her face, his voice sharpened. "What is it, Jan?"

She shook her head wordlessly. Now that the danger was past, she was no longer at her ease with him. Too much lay between them. She knew she owed him some explanation for the need to save her life, but she was too exhausted, too emotionally buffeted, to embark on it.

Roger didn't press for an answer. Instead, he said quietly, "I'm taking you and the children straight to my parents. You need to get away from this place. Don't worry," he added, seeing her movement of protest, "I shan't be there myself. I really have business to attend to, and I'll be based in London with my colleagues."

Jan said awkwardly, "It's not only that. I do want to see your parents, of course, but not just yet. I can't possibly leave Lady Peel till Rowena gets back."

"Whyever not?" He sounded impatient, suspecting an excuse.

"Roger, she's devoted to Miles. He's like a son to her. And—well, certain facts are going to come to light about Sir Reginald, which won't be easy for her, either."

"I can't pretend to understand all this. I just go cold, wondering what'd have happened if I hadn't turned up when I did."

"I know." She looked up at him. "Surely your mother told you we were staying here? Why did you go to Rylands?"

He shrugged. "You might have moved back. I decided to try there first, and luckily the door was on the latch."

As she'd left it for the children. Jan shuddered, remembering her terror for them. They'd recovered more quickly than she had. Excitement and a sense of importance had quickly banished their fear, and they were at the moment working their way through a large lunch, watched over solicitously by Edith.

Lady Peel was up in her room. Jan had told her as gently as she could about Miles, and the old lady made little comment. "I'll stay here quietly for a while," she said, "and give you a chance to talk to your husband. But when the police arrive, I'll come down to see them."

It wasn't till Jan had left her that she realized Lady Peel was probably unaware that they'd separated.

Roger, who'd been watching the expressions on her face, broke into her thoughts. "We've the hell of a lot of talking to do."

Jan closed her eyes wearily. Not now, she thought, please not now. And as if in answer, the doorbell rang through the house. The police had arrived.

In Webb's absence, it was Chief Inspector Horn, accompanied by WDS Lucas, who came to Cajabamba. Jan was glad that at least the woman detective was known to her. The Chief Inspector looked forbidding, with a hooked nose and shaggy dark hair, but he was a kindly man, and gentle with them.

Jan braced herself to repeat Miles's involved story. If he denied what he'd told her, the burden of accusation would rest on her. But to some extent, Horn forestalled her.

"We were on our way to Mr. Coady when the call came through," he told them. "We'd tried to contact him without success all day yesterday."

As had Jan herself. "You mean you knew it was him?"

"We had a strong suspicion, yes, but the real break came this morning with a phone call from a Mr. Plaidy, who's an art historian. He's just back from two weeks in Italy, and only learned of Marriott's death on his return. It was a considerable shock, because it was he who'd asked Marriott to investigate Mr. Coady."

"Investigate?" Lady Peel said sharply.

"Only as a journalist, ma'am. It seems he'd recognized some prints which appeared under Mr. Coady's name—he'd seen them as a boy, in one of the Stately Homes. But he'd no proof of forgery, so, since he knew Marriott slightly, he asked him to look into it. And thereby sent him to his death."

Jan drew a deep breath. At least hers wasn't the only testimony.

"So your colleagues needn't have gone to Peru after all." Lady Peel was sitting up very straight, and Jan wondered at her composure. But there was still another blow in store for her. Gently, the Chief Inspector, who had read Laurence Coady's letter, prepared her for it.

"It wasn't a wasted journey, ma'am. Perhaps you're forgetting the sequins and the bandage."

The old lady stared at him, and her face paled. "The third expedition?"

"Exactly. When the police arrived after Mr. Coverdale's call, they found valuable items concealed behind the wardrobe."

The old eyes found Jan's. "The Punchao and necklace?"

She nodded. "They didn't steal them," she said quickly, "there's a perfectly good explanation. I'll show you my father's letter. Roger brought it from home."

"But I don't understand. How did this concern Mr. Marriott?"

"I'd like to know that myself," Horn admitted wryly. "Perhaps Mrs. Coverdale can explain?"

Reluctantly, Jan did so: Miles's visit to the sick-room, his row with Edward and Rowena, the childish vindictiveness of the guy. Finally, his voice still echoing in her ears, she told of the association of ideas which led to his dressing Marriott's body in the discarded dummy's clothes.

There was a long silence when she'd finished. Then Horn said softly, "So that's it. No wonder it had us foxed; we'd two separate crimes on our hands, with entirely different motives. All along we'd assumed Marriott's death was directly linked with the bandage, sequins and wallet, whereas they were merely props which happened to be on hand."

Jan, who'd been anxiously watching Lady Peel, saw the old lady sway, and slipping to the ground beside her, she took hold of her hands.

"You do understand?" she asked gently. "They only did what they had to. It nearly destroyed them."

The glazed eyes came down to her face. "Reggie and the others? Yes, I see that. But Miles—I feel responsible for him. He was put in my charge."

"His mother was unbalanced," Jan said, "and Miles was flawed, too. You mustn't blame yourself; there was nothing you could have done."

It was three weeks later. As the plane rose higher, the tiny figures of Edward and Rowena grew indistinguishable, lost in the vastness of the city spread below.

Jan leaned back and closed her eyes, letting the events of those last weeks drift through her mind. As promised, she had stayed at Cajabamba till Edward and Rowena returned from Peru, when the whole story had to be gone through again. She'd noticed a new gentleness in Rowena's attitude to her mother. Perhaps now Miles was no longer between them, they'd come closer together.

As for the treasure, it would soon be on its way to Peru. Jan hoped Quispe Tupac would have understood, realized that, in the museum, his own people would have a chance to see it.

Nor had the last week with Roger's parents been easy. Though he must have warned them not to question her, their obvious anxiety about her marriage added to her own stress.

And now she was on her way home, with the problems she'd run away from still awaiting her.

She sighed, then, seeing Julie's concerned glance, managed a smile. "Glad to be going home?"

The child nodded. "It's cold in England." She paused. "Is Daddy coming back to live with us?"

Jan glanced at Roger across the aisle, knowing from his tenseness that he'd heard the question. They'd had little time for private discussion, but he'd made it clear his brief affair was over, that he'd known it was a mistake from the moment he left home.

"You'd better ask him," she said quietly. The child turned to her father, and over her head, Jan's eyes held his. It would take time to readjust to each other, to bury the hurt, but she knew now that she wanted to try. She waited as tensely as her daughter for his reply.

"If you'll all have me," he said.